THE
HISTORY
OF
AMERICAN
NURSING

Edited by
Susan Reverby, Wellesley College

A GARLAND SERIES

AMERICAN NURSES IN FICTION
An Anthology of Short Stories

Edited with an introduction by
Barbara Melosh

GARLAND PUBLISHING, INC.
NEW YORK • LONDON
1984

For a complete list of the titles in this series see the final pages
of this volume.

Copyright © 1984 by Barbara Melosh

Library of Congress Cataloging in Publication Data
Main entry under title:

American nurses in fiction.

   (The History of American nursing)
   1. Short stories, American.   2. Nurses—United States—
Fiction.   3. American fiction—20th century.   I. Melosh,
Barbara. II. Series.
PS648.N87A48   1984   813'.01'08352613   83-49120
ISBN 0-8240-6518-2 (alk. paper)

The volumes in this series are printed on acid-free, 250-year-
life paper.

Printed in the United States of America

Contents

Introduction

Nurse characters appear in surprising profusion in the pages of American fiction, perhaps better represented than any other group of women workers. Their various guises reveal much about the complex cultural meanings that surround nurses and nursing. Portraits of nurses as nurturing mothers or sympathetic allies identify nurses as ideal women, drawing parallels between the nurse's care of her patient and the mother's devotion to her child. In other characterizations, nurses are depicted as "unnatural" women whose authority and expertise set them beyond the borders of proper femininity: they are shown as icy martinets or sexual predators, threats to male prerogatives. Sometimes the nurse is the emblem of the outsider, a pathetic spinster or strange recluse. And other stories reveal the nurse as an initiate into esoteric secrets: her knowledge of the body and her proximity to feared illness and death draw her into the worlds of forbidden sexuality, human frailty and evil, and supernatural perception. These diverse portrayals share a single common element—in all, the nurse's sex is a critical element of her professional identity.

Ben Ames Williams's "The Nurse" and Dorothy Parker's "Horsie" both depict private duty nurses who live vicariously through their patients. Williams's story is a character sketch of an officious practical nurse, Millie, a middle-aged woman whose life revolves around "her" babies. In this sentimental and condescending portrait, Millie's absorption in her work is the measure of her marginality. The story holds us at a calculated distance from the pathos of a lonely woman, partly exploiting the pity that this character evokes but also containing it by poking fun at Millie's self-important stance. In "Horsie," Dorothy Parker conveys a more complex and critical view, using humor to expose the pretensions of class. Told from the viewpoint of the nurse's employer, Gerald Kruger, the story begins by enlisting the same amused condescension that sets the tone in Williams's sketch: Kruger dubs the nurse "Horsie" as he and his spoiled wife laugh privately over her awkward efforts to fit into their carelessly wealthy household. By the end of the story, Parker has deftly turned the humor around, bringing the reader to sympathize with Horsie and to look critically on the superficial Krugers. The two authors deploy humor for different purposes, but they both proceed from the common ground of a recognizable type: the lonely woman who makes her work a substitute for friendship, romantic love, and family.

Conrad Aiken's "Bring! Bring!" also works from the premise of the nurse's social marginality, but his story explores the illicit freedom of an outsider. The opening scene sets the mood of languid sexuality as Nurse Rooker remembers her dream of the night before: rocking on a boat, she laughs with a lover who uncorks a foaming bottle of champagne. An atmosphere of decadent wealth surrounds the household where the nurse has come to care for a passive female patient. The sea murmurs, circling birds seem to cry "Bring! Bring!," and the nurse's employer, her patient's husband, carries on an affair. Treated like a servant by both her patient and her employer's imperious lover, the nurse watches, waits; and finally wins her own triumph by luring the husband into a new sexual alliance. The story is told from the vantage point of the nurse's intermediate position in the household: neither wife nor social equal, she has access to intimate family secrets and the license to take the initiative.

Ellen Glasgow's "The Shadowy Third," a ghost story, also uses the atmospheric possibilities of private duty to good effect. In addition, her story further develops the nurse protagonist. The conflict between obedience to the doctor and loyalty to the patient, a classic dilemma for nurses, becomes the fulcrum of the plot. Margaret Randolph is a recently graduated nurse; she stands at the edge of the professional world. In the beginning of the story, she is flattered when a prominent surgeon requests her services for his wife. When the nurse first enters the physician's house, she sees a little girl, only to find soon after that the child is dead. Like her grieving patient, she has glimpsed the ghost of the woman's daughter, her child by another marriage. Gradually uncovering the secret of the household, the nurse comes to suspect that the revered doctor has murdered this child. Her experience forces her to weigh the claims of empathy versus scientific knowledge, the spirit versus the body. As a woman, she is allied with the world of emotion and intuition, represented by the sad mother and her ghost child; as a nurse, she belongs to the world of rational thought and objectivity. In the course of the story, she must choose between these opposing modes of perception and experience.

"When It Happens," by James Hopper, brings a sophisticated twist to the cliché of a male patient infatuated with his female nurse. The narrator, a writer, recounts his old friend's story of a recent hospital stay. In the telling, Sam Nolan (the patient) repeatedly denies that he has fallen in love with his young private nurse, Marjorie Downe; as he keeps insisting, he only wants to help his writer friend to understand "how it happens when it happens." Sam tells the story to try to explain away his experience: during his hospital stay, he has teetered on the brink of a difficult truth about his unrewarding marriage and squandered talents. We never see the real nurse behind the protagonist's idealized vision. Instead, Hopper skillfully reveals the infatuation as Sam's wistful longing for lost innocence, his regret for the unrealized possibilities of his own youth.

Ring Lardner's "Zone of Quiet" and Frederick Hazlitt Brennan's "Nurse's Choice" both make light-hearted use of the stock character of the frivolous young nurse. The humorous "Zone of Quiet" is told from the viewpoint of a wry middle-aged male patient at the mercy of his talkative private nurse. As he recovers from an operation, he is the amused if weary audience for tales of her lively social life. The story's comedy lies in Lardner's unerring ear for casual speech: the breathless monologue of the flapper-nurse carries the whole narrative. We laugh because we can see through her self-deceptions, using the nurse's own account of events to stay one step ahead of her. In Brennan's "Nurse's Choice," the protagonist, we are told gaily, faces the central dilemma of a young nurse—a decision of the heart. Forced to choose between two young doctors, the nurse picks her man when the two suitors perform an emergency appendectomy on her. In the resolution, she weighs the virtues of professional objectivity against the transports of romantic love, with the predictable outcome.

Neither story focuses directly on nursing, and yet their hospital settings are more than incidental. Lardner's humor works partly because the story taps the underlying unease that hospitals evoke; he converts the fear of illness and dependency into laughter. By placing his frivolous young woman in the serious role of a nurse, Lardner broadens his caricature of this type. Similarly, the situation of illness sharpens the contrast between the young woman and the middle-aged man by reversing the expected relationships of deference and authority and closing the social distance between them. Stripped of his customary prerogatives by illness, the male patient, older and wiser, is thrown into a helpless intimacy with and dependence on his social inferior, the young, empty-headed female nurse. In "Nurse's Choice," the hospital atmosphere adds novelty to the familiar "boy-meets-girl" plot; at the same time, the likeable characters and frothy story render the hospital more familiar and accessible to a lay audience. The perennial popularity of hospital settings suggests the appeal of these glimpses behind the scene. Stories like this reassure us that, beneath their formidable competence and seeming impersonality, doctors and nurses are only human after all.

From Ken Kesey's "Big Nurse" to "Hot Lips" of M*A*S*H fame, the autocratic head nurse is another common fixture of fictional wards. Arthur Gordon's "Old Ironpuss" sympathetically portrays a gruff nurse, showing us the heart of gold and the professional wisdom underneath her brusque manner. By the end of the story, we admire the older nurse's unsung devotion to her patients. But the cost of her professional commitment is social isolation. Gordon's character counterpoints the frivolous nurses in "Zone of Quiet" and "Nurse's Choice": together, the stories suggest an irreconcilable conflict between serious work and "femininity."

"A Drink of Water," by T. K. Brown III, manipulates the psychological associations of nursing and illness in a grotesque and yet oddly compelling story of female betrayal. Fred MacCann, blind and limbless after a war injury, is condemned to relive the dependency of infancy. His rescuer, the gentle nurse Alice, collaborates in Fred's fantasies of her as the ideal woman. At first she acts the part of the selfless mother; as the story unfolds, she becomes his seducer and lover. But in the denouement, we see that Alice is neither ideal mother nor true lover, but instead a woman as damaged as her helpless patient. A classic of fifties' misogyny, the story exploits many layers of ambivalence about women, seen both as objects of desire and as threats to autonomy. The selection of the hospital setting and nurse protagonist is critical to the story's emotional intensity. Fred's terrible dependency lends credence to the exploration of infantile fantasy—both the desire to fuse with the mother and the fear of being incorporated—and creates a plausible setting for a character cast in the image of the devouring mother.

What can we learn about nurses from these stories? These writers are not intent on making a statement about nurses and nursing; their fictions cannot be read as direct commentaries. Nor can we use fiction as a measure of public opinion. A short story is not a Gallup poll, and it is risky to extrapolate from the perspective of a story to the assumptions and beliefs of its audience. Nonetheless, we can interpret the artistic selection that shapes these fictions. In each story, we can ask—why nurses? How do the authors use nurse characters to build their images, associations, and emotions? What would readers need to know about nurses to make the characters intelligible; what would they need to believe to make them convincing? And finally, what place do nurses occupy in the moral universe of the fiction? Read in this way—as fictions made credible by their correspondences to the world we know—short stories reveal a glimpse of the cultural categories that inform both literature and social life.

Nurses concerned about their public images will find little comfort in these stories. Even the most positive portrayals, such as Glasgow's engaging Margaret Randolph, focus on the nurse as a woman rather than on the work of nursing. We gain little sense of nurses' relationships with medical or nursing colleagues, little idea of their daily routines or the special skills and knowledge of their work. Instead, nurse characters are used to magnify issues of gender and sexual conflict: they are good mothers and loyal sisters, sexual temptresses and devouring lovers. Significantly, in the three stories that give us the closest look at nurses' work—Williams's "The Nurse," Parker's "Horsie," and Gordon's "Old Ironpuss"—nurses are explicitly depicted as sexless; they are lonely and eccentric women whose work is a pathetic substitute for the unattainable satisfactions of love. Hopper's "When It Happens" is the most self-conscious in its view of the symbolism associated with nurses: the author examines the male patient's perceptions of his nurse as a projection of his fantasy. Ironically, though, it is only here, in the realm of wish-fulfillment, that the good nurse is also a Real Woman.

These fictions testify to the enduring sense of anomaly with which our culture regards working women. Inadvertently, they also suggest the intertwined fates of nursing and the women's movement. Until gender is no longer such a consequential category, and womanhood such a pronounced disadvantage in the world of work, nurses will be seen first as women and only secondarily as workers.

THE NURSE

A STORY

BY BEN AMES WILLIAMS

THERE is a curious institution, widely distributed, called the waiting room. You will find specimens almost everywhere, in railroad stations, in hotels, in department stores, and in business offices of every description. The waiting room is a fearful thing. At best it offers boredom, and at the worst it is a place where one sits through minutes that seem interminable, filled with apprehension or with despair.

Millie had had some experience of waiting rooms, and she dreaded them. She had been sitting in this particular waiting room at the employment agency for three days. She was a little woman, one of those women whose appearance suggests that they have been wrung dry by the torque and torsion of their own emotions; a little woman thin and taut and just now curiously tremulous. She was probably about forty-five years old and she sat among the others without taking any part in the occasional passages of conversation among them. She seemed to be unconscious of their presence, and her eyes, inflamed and weary, looked blankly straight before her. And sometimes, for no apparent reason, they became suffused with tears; not merely misted with moisture, but drowned in a swimming, drenching flood which flowed over her lids and down her dry cheeks until she remembered to wipe away these evidences of the grief which racked her.

On her first day, when she had tried to talk with a prospective employer, she had been unable to control her voice; and her eyes had thus gushed tears till the other woman said impatiently:

"Well, I certainly don't want you if you're the crying kind," and turned away.

Millie had then been rather relieved than disappointed. She always dreaded this necessity of seeking new employment while she was still in the throes of her latest loss. So she sat all that day and the next and into the third. And whenever it appeared that she must talk with one of those who came here seeking servants, she averted her eyes, weakly endeavoring to avoid attracting their notice, willing to put off the inevitable adventure of new employment.

But on the third day she found herself replying in a dull voice to the questions put to her by a woman, perhaps thirty years old, who introduced herself by a name which Millie scarcely heard. She was not interested in the names of her mistresses; she had had so many of them. They were a shadowy procession in the background of her life, those in the past no more definite in her mind than those who waited for her in the future. This woman's name might have been Smith or Brown. It happened to be Mrs. Jones.

Millie answered her questions in a dull and lifeless tone, telling as impersonally as though she spoke of someone else what her life had been. She had been a baby nurse since she was seventeen years old. It would be hard to pack into one sentence a more tragic biography. A woman who has loved one baby and lost it wears forever after in

Reprinted from *Harper's* 152 (April 1926), pp. 549–557

her eyes the mark of her grief like a pale flower. But Millie had been condemned by life to love many babies and to lose them all.

Mrs. Jones asked question upon question, but Millie asked only one. "Is it a boy or a girl?"

"A little girl," Mrs. Jones replied, and Millie's ravaged face seemed to lighten faintly at the word.

"I always like the girls best," she confessed.

They arranged for Millie to come the next morning to take the place, and Millie was for the rest of that day a little more cheerful. Her aching grief found anodyne in the prospect of having another baby to love.

There is hardly another ordeal comparable to that of entering the home of strangers and finding yourself there at once an alien, an outsider, liable to instant dismissal, and at the same time in such an intimate relation to the life of the family as that held by the baby nurse. Millie was still sick with sorrow over the loss of her last baby, a loss as irrevocable and a grief as poignant as though the baby had died. But she had no more tears, and she entered this new household, hiding her misery behind a stony countenance.

Mrs. Jones was a friendly, kindly young woman, competent, sure of what she wanted, and at once firm and conciliatory. She was just out of the hospital, and there was still a trained nurse in the house. The little girl who was to be Millie's baby now was about six weeks old.

"Her name is Joan," Mrs. Jones explained to Millie. "This is her room, and you will use this bathroom, and you can keep her things on these shelves, and you will sleep here across the hall."

Millie, with every desire in the world to conciliate her new mistress, nevertheless found herself saying in an exacting tone:

"I always want to sleep in the room with my babies, so I can hear them in the night."

Mrs. Jones nodded willingly enough.

"If you prefer, that is quite all right," she assented. "I will have a cot put in here for you; but I think by the time Joan is three months old we can give up her night feedings altogether. We did with Johnnie."

Millie had already seen Johnnie, the son of the house, about six years old and a lively youngster. Although she had an infinite and understanding tenderness for little babies, she had long since learned that when they grew old enough to walk and to talk they began to escape from her. She knew that she could not, as the saying is, "get along with older children"; and she asked Mrs. Jones now:

"Do you want I should take care of Johnnie too?"

"He can dress himself," Mrs. Jones said proudly. "And he sleeps all night, and he has breakfast and lunch with us. Charles gives him his supper, and he goes to bed before our dinner. I will want you to keep his room in order; but you won't have much to do with him."

"I like to give all my time to my baby," Millie explained, and Mrs. Jones agreed:

"You'll have very little else to do."

The trained nurse left the next day, and Millie threw herself at once into the interminable routine of petty tasks which the care of a small baby brings in its train. Mrs. Jones had been unable to nurse the child more than two weeks, so that Joan was already on the bottle. Millie roused at about half-past five every morning, heated the first bottle over the small electric plate in the bathroom, and held it while Joan absorbed its contents. Afterwards the baby slept for an hour or more, while Millie had time to dress, to have her breakfast in the kitchen with Charles and Laura, and to do some of the enormous amount of washing which had to be done every day. At eight o'clock she took Joan up and bathed her.

Another bottle, another sleep, another waking and another bottle, fresh clothing, and so to sleep again. Thus the recurring days.

In the care of Joan, Millie was perfectly and passionately happy; but not in her other relations. From the beginning she disliked young Johnnie so definitely that at times her feeling amounted to hatred. He was, of course, disorderly, and even though she might be tired and her back might be aching, it was necessary for her to busy herself about his room, forever putting back in their places things which he as continually threw into confusion again. Also, he was noisy, and whenever his shrill voice was upraised she expected him to wake Joan; and if she was near enough, she always tried to command him to silence. But the second or third time this occurred, Mrs. Jones reproved her.

"You must expect Johnnie to be noisy, Millie," she told the nurse.

"He'll wake my baby," Millie jealously retorted.

Mrs. Jones smiled a little, and said, "I'm afraid we're a noisy household. Joan will have to get used to living with us. You mustn't keep hushing Johnnie. After all, he has his rights as well as Joan."

Millie was silenced, because she knew by experience that those considerations which seemed to her so overwhelming would have no weight with her mistress; and her position was weak, since Joan was from the first a sound sleeper, quite undisturbed by anything that went on in the big house. But the fact that Joan never did waken could not prevent Millie's being constantly afraid she would, and a remonstrance at Johnnie's noise was forever on the tip of her tongue.

There were many other disturbing sounds in the house, and they all jarred on her taut nerves; so that after each burst of laughter, or cry, or concussion of a slamming door, she would sit tensely listening for long seconds, expecting a wail of distress from the room where Joan was sleeping.

It did not matter what the source of these noises might be, she resented them all equally. When Johnnie was to blame she was furious; and when older folk were responsible her anger was even more intense. One night two guests came in to dinner and, since the weather was bad, Mr. and Mrs. Jones insisted that they stay over night. When the four of them came upstairs to go to bed, there was a good deal of talking and laughing in the halls; and Millie's anger overcame her prudence so that she put on her dressing gown, and—an absurd little figure with her small braid hanging between her shoulders—she came out into the hall and faced them with burning eyes, and said sharply:

"Joan has just gone to sleep. You'll have to keep quiet. I can't have her waked up now."

Mr. Jones himself replied sternly, "She never wakes, Millie. And even if she did, she cannot expect us to go whispering about the house all the time." He was a large man, his very bulk impressive, and Millie hated him as much as she feared him. But she dared make no reply and retreated to her own room full of bitter rage.

She soon found herself involved in continual discord with Charles, the house man who did the chores and served the meals, and with Laura, his wife, the cook. Millie had her meals with them in the kitchen, and it seemed to her that they were extravagant in their use of electricity and gas, and that they wasted food. The great love which she always gave her babies left in her nothing but angry resentment at the rest of the world; and, although she knew from experience that only trouble could come from any altercation between her and the other servants, she was unable to refrain from criticizing their methods to them and to Mrs. Jones.

Mrs. Jones at first received these reports without comment; but the situation became more and more acute until she was compelled at last to silence Millie and to bid her attend to her own work and let the others attend to theirs.

"You are here to take care of Joan, Millie," she said definitely. "I do not ask you to supervise Charles and Laura. That is my business. They do their work and you do yours, and what they do or how they do it does not concern you."

Millie, knowing the danger in such a course, nevertheless could not refrain from a protesting word. "I can't have them wasting electric light the way they do," she said stridently. And Mrs. Jones replied:

"If you can't be happy here, Millie, you are perfectly free to go at any time; but I will not have you interfering with the other servants."

Millie made no reply. At this word, this suggestion of her leaving, she had been struck with such stark terror that she could not speak. At this time she had been only about two months in the Jones household. In the normal course of events she might expect to stay until Joan was two years old, and there was always a chance that another baby might appear in the meantime to prolong her sojourn. To leave now, while Joan was still small, would be to lose her baby; and she could not bear to contemplate that possibility. Already Joan had ascended to that throne in her heart which so many babies had occupied before. They had become shades, shadows of lost loved ones in the background of her thoughts; but Joan was alive, actual, twelve or fourteen pounds of substantial, tangible, sweet flesh; and she began already to know Millie, to look forward to her appearances, and to respond to her caresses and endearments with wide and toothless smiles.

This is the tragedy of the baby nurse, that she loves her baby so completely that she will endure anything human flesh can endure, rather than be separated from her charge. Millie would go to any length to avoid this catastrophe; and that afternoon, in a desperate desire to placate Mrs. Jones and to ameliorate the impatience which the other might be feeling, she made a cup of tea and took it up to her mistress with an apologetic word.

"I thought you might like it," she explained.

And Mrs. Jones thanked her, and the world was thereafter for a while serene.

Millie's life during the next few months was a succession of irritating incidents from which she found escape in the hours she spent with the baby. Joan now slept less. Her night feedings had been abandoned. She had bottles four times a day; and from about seven o'clock in the morning till the ten o'clock bottle, and from the two o'clock bottle until that which she had at six, she was awake. In the morning Millie brought her downstairs to sit in the dining room while Mr. and Mrs. Jones and Johnnie had their breakfast. In the afternoon she took the baby for a walk in her perambulator and stayed away from the house, when the weather was fair, as late as it was possible, reveling in the long hours alone with Joan. But she could not always be with her baby, and in her relations with Charles and Laura and with Johnnie there were continual irritations.

Between her and Charles there was a continuing feud. Charles was devoted to Johnnie, and he so contrived his time as to be able to help the little boy dress in the morning and undress at night. The two were boon companions. But Millie hated Johnnie, and he returned this feeling not with hatred, because he was too young to feel that passion, but with resentment of her attentions and with an inclination to become fretful and angry at her ministrations. She hated Johnnie; but the fact that he welcomed Charles and liked to be with the man aroused in Millie an infuriating jealousy. Sometimes she and Charles became involved in arguments as to the simple business of keeping Johnnie's room in order; and it seemed to Millie that Charles encouraged Johnnie to rebel at her authority and to be impudent to her.

One morning when she brought Joan to the dining room she had had such a passage with the man, and it had so wrought upon her nerves that she was in tears. When she came in, Mr. and Mrs. Jones and Johnnie were already at the table; and she burst out in explosive complaint, hating herself for doing it, knowing the risk she ran, yet unable to control her tongue. With tears streaming down her face she cried: "Mrs. Jones, I want you to tell Johnnie that he isn't to talk back to me the way he does."

Mrs. Jones said quietly, "We'll discuss that by and by, Millie."

"He won't do anything I tell him to," Millie insisted. "And him and Charles just laugh at me."

Charles, coming in just then with the coffee, was driven to self-defense.

"Johnnie's all right, Mrs. Jones," he said stoutly. "She won't let him alone. She don't understand boys. I can take care of Johnnie all right if she'd just leave him alone."

Mrs. Jones said decisively, "That will do, Charles!"

"Yes, ma'am," Charles agreed and left the room.

But Millie, unutterably exasperated, cried again, "Johnnie's got to be made to behave, ma'am."

Mrs. Jones repeated, "We'll discuss that later, Millie!"

And Millie, though she was almost beside herself with weeping rage, felt the menace in the other's tone and left the room.

After her husband had gone, Mrs. Jones summoned Millie and said to her steadily: "You are not to do such a thing as that again, Millie. I don't want Mr. Jones bothered by anything that goes on at home. If you have anything to say to me, wait until he has gone and come to me quietly."

Millie cried, "Well, I can't stand the way Johnnie treats me."

"Hereafter," Mrs. Jones told her, "you need have no contact with Johnnie except to keep his room in order. Charles will take care of him, and I am sure you will get along all right if you avoid trouble with Johnnie or with Charles."

"I can't stand it," Millie cried.

"If you can't be happy here with us," Mrs. Jones told her, "I would rather you did not stay. I don't want anyone in the house who is unhappy."

The words struck Millie with a sobering effect, as though Mrs. Jones had dashed cold water in her face. They silenced her utterly, and drove her from the room to fight down all that day her desperate fear. That afternoon she made Mrs. Jones another cup of tea.

She thought Joan the most beautiful of babies and she thought of Joan always as her baby, and Joan seemed to Millie to feel that Millie was her whole world, too. When Millie came to her in the morning, even before the nurse entered the room Joan was apt to begin to crow with delight at her coming. And when Millie bathed her, changed her garments, talked to her in that cheering, reassuring tone which, no matter what her own mood, she was always able to summon for Joan, Joan fairly wriggled with delight. When in the morning it came time for Mr. Jones to go to town and Millie was summoned to take the baby, Joan always came to her eagerly. And sometimes when either Mr. or Mrs. Jones offered to take the baby from Millie, Joan would laugh aloud, and throw her arms around Millie's neck and snuggle her face into the nurse's shoulder as though it were a game which she played.

Millie used to nurse the memory of these scenes, and to tell herself over and over that Joan loved her more than she loved either her father or her mother; and thus thinking, she would hug Joan with a fierce tenderness full of passion. At such times Joan chuckled and babbled with delight as though these ferocious caresses were delightful to her. Millie reveled in these hours when she had Joan to herself, the rest of the world apart. But at those moments when she perceived that Joan had passed from one of the phases of babyhood to another, abandoning one little trick for the next, Millie felt a poignant alarm at the approach of the time when Joan would no longer be a baby at all and so would escape from her.

She stifled these forebodings, clinging to the present, refusing to consider the future, blinding herself to the inevitable end of all this happiness, insistently declining to look forward to the day when—one way or another—she would lose this baby, whom she loved, as she had lost so many before. Yet these fears, though they were stifled, had their effect upon her; her furtive dread sharpened her tongue, and she found herself saying and doing irritating things. At such moments she was full of regret, regret not so much because of what she had done as because by such actions she laid herself open to dismissal, ran the risk of losing Joan. And afterwards she would seek to make amends, throwing herself into her work with new zeal, seeking tasks outside her appointed duties, paying her mistress small attentions, bringing her a potted plant, making a dress for Joan, or serving Mrs. Jones a cup of tea in the afternoon.

Thus her life was a succession of crimes and repentances, a series of passions each followed by fearful remorse. And there were days, occasionally weeks, when she held such a rigid bridle upon her tongue that her silence made her seem sulky; and there were other days when the check which she kept upon herself slipped, and she loosed in bitter words the blind and venomous anger which she felt against the whole world.

Once or twice she caught herself talking to Charles and Laura of Mr. and Mrs. Jones in terms frankly slanderous, and for days thereafter she was full of bitter and terrified self-reproach, moving cautiously, watching the demeanor of her mistress for any sign that her words had been reported, shrinking with fear of the destruction she had invited. She was her own worst enemy and she knew this as well as anyone, but it became more and more difficult for her to keep a curb upon her tongue.

As Joan approached her first birthday, half a dozen influences combined to produce a cumulative nervous strain which Millie found more and more tormenting. For one thing the baby was maturing. Millie had wished to keep her as long as possible completely helpless and dependent, so she had prisoned her in her crib or in her perambulator, and Joan had not yet learned to creep. But Mrs. Jones at last insisted that Millie put the baby on the floor for an hour or two a day, to exercise those muscles which were ready to assume their functions.

The result was an increasingly rapid development of Joan's powers. She set herself to the task of learning to manipulate her small body with a persistency as deliberate as though she were quite conscious of what she did. And she would sit up on the floor, pull herself forward over her legs until she lay on her face, push herself back up to a sitting posture again, pull herself forward once more and roll on her back, and from this position again push herself up until she was sitting erect, following this routine over and over as though she had been set these tasks to do. She began also to exercise her voice, no longer in the meaningless outcries of infancy, but trying different tones, now shrill, now guttural; and some of these utterances assumed a form suggestive of speech, till it was easy to imagine she was trying to say something.

Millie had cared for so many babies that she knew what these signs portended She knew that Joan would soon escape from her ministering care, and this knowledge oppressed her dreams.

The nurse was also at this time under

an increased physical strain. Mrs. Jones was planning a birthday party for Joan, to which half a dozen other babies, a little younger or a little older, would be invited. Millie decided to make a dress which Joan should wear on that occasion; and into this work she threw all her energies, spending upon it every hour not directly devoted to Joan herself, working at it in the early morning, at moments snatched during the day, and late at night when she might better have been asleep. The result was that she was tired almost all the time, and this weariness served to break down in large and larger measure her self-control, till she was in continual conflict within herself, fighting to stifle the resentment which she felt against those among whom her life was cast.

There had long existed between her and Charles a state of open warfare; and this was brought to something like a crisis one evening when Mr. and Mrs. Jones had gone out to dinner. Charles, as he liked to do on such occasions, had put the young son of the house to bed. Millie was moved by some blind and senseless impulse, after Charles had gone downstairs, to get Johnnie up again and insist upon giving him a bath.

The little boy felt the injustice of this. "I don't want to take a bath," he cried.

"You're dirty," Millie told him. "You ought to be ashamed to go to bed as dirty as you are; and Charles ought to be ashamed to let you. Now you come right along into the bathroom and Millie will give you a nice bath."

"I had a bath this morning," Johnnie insisted bitterly. "I'm not going to take a bath now."

Millie's tone was soothing, yet there was in it at the same time something acidly venomous.

"Come right along," she retorted. "There's no use fussing. You've got to have a bath the way Millie says."

Johnnie still resisting, she undertook to compel him; but the result was such an outcry that Charles heard and came

swiftly upstairs, and there followed a bitter altercation between the two servants, Johnnie clinging to Charles for protection, Millie reduced to a state of blind and incoherent frenzy.

But there was no way she could carry her point, since Charles was quite obviously the physical master of the situation. She surrendered because she had to surrender; but the episode remained in her mind and accentuated the developing enmity between her and Charles to such a point that the least incident was sufficient to set them into open wrangling. Millie, out of necessity, ate in the kitchen with Charles and Laura, and it is not to be wondered at that under the circumstances she had no relish for her meals, and her digestion suffered.

Yet still she tried desperately to control herself, to avoid giving further offense to her mistress in any way. But the very desperation of her efforts in this direction led her into error. Millie's greatest virtue had always been that she gave her babies perfect care; but now, once and then again, she was guilty of negligence even toward Joan. The first occasion followed a night when she had worked late upon the dress for Joan's birthday party, and her resultant weariness made her oversleep the hour for the morning bottle. The baby awoke and cried, and Millie did not even hear till Mrs. Jones came to her door. Millie's bitter self-reproach translated itself into anger against her mistress. She said sharply:

"You don't have to come after me. I heard her. She's all right to cry a little while. I'll get to her in a minute. You can't expect me to keep on the run all the time."

Mrs. Jones hesitated, as though to control her voice, but she only said:

"You had better take her up now, Millie. I don't want her to cry when it isn't necessary," and turned away.

The final incident occurred one afternoon when she was about to take Joan out for a ride in her perambulator.

Joan was by this time more and more vigorous and active, and when Millie put her in the baby carriage she did not buckle the safety strap sufficiently tight. She went back into the house to get her own hat and coat and while she was gone Joan, wriggling this way and that, managed to twist herself till she was hanging half out of the carriage and forthwith began to scream with fright and despair.

As luck would have it, Charles heard her and ran out from the kitchen in time to avoid any serious result from the mishap. But Millie also had heard Joan crying and was only a second behind Charles; and the fact that he had interfered seemed to her so bitter a wrong that she upbraided him violently.

"Take your hands off my baby," she cried in a shrill and exasperated voice. "I won't have you touching her. I won't have you bothering her."

Charles said sternly, "It's lucky I did touch her. She'd have bumped her head. You ought to take more care the way you buckle her in."

"I don't need any man to tell me how to take care of babies," Millie screamed at him. "You get back into your kitchen, you scullery maid."

Charles laughed shortly. "Hard names never hurt anybody," he retorted. "If they did, I could think up one or two myself."

But the fact that he stood his ground, as though passing judgment upon the manner in which she now bestowed Joan in the perambulator, whetted Millie's anger to a pitch near delirium; and when Mrs. Jones, attracted by the sound of the nurse's shrill and frenzied voice, came to the door, Millie was in a perfect paroxysm of fury.

The result of this culminating incident was her dismissal.

"If you can't control yourself," Mrs. Jones said in a tone of finality, "I can't let you be about Joan any longer. I'm sorry, Millie, but you will have to go. I'll have a taxi come for you at three this afternoon."

Millie cried all that day, not silently, but with wild and explosive sounds, the tears streaming from her eyes. She at first accepted her dismissal without argument, but when Mrs. Jones insisted upon bathing Joan herself, and told Millie to go to her room and pack her things, the old woman for the first time fully realized that sentence had been passed upon her. Her agony of spirit was like that of a man condemned to death; and when Joan was asleep—for even now Millie would not do anything calculated to disturb the routine of the baby's life—the nurse went to Mrs. Jones' room and sought to bring about a change in the other's decision. Her abject grief, the craven pleadings to which in the end she was at last driven, worked upon her mistress intolerably; and there was a moment when one of these women was almost as unhappy as the other. But although she perceived how much of a tragedy this was to Millie, Mrs. Jones had made her decision and was strong enough to hold to it.

"I've only kept you so long," she said, "because you've been so good to Joan. You're a good nurse, Millie, but you're a most uncomfortable person to have around. If you would learn to be civil and to attend to your own affairs, you'd avoid so much trouble. I've made up my mind. I'll have to let you go."

Millie left the house in mid-afternoon. As her belongings were being packed into the taxi-cab which Mrs. Jones had summoned, she wept unbearably, and Mrs. Jones could not refrain from asking:

"Where do you plan to go, Millie?"

Millie said desperately, "I'll go somewhere. I don't know where."

"Shall I send you to a hotel till you can get another place?" Mrs. Jones suggested, and Millie shook her head

"No," she replied. And she named a woman whom she knew and said, "I'll go to her house for a day or two."

When she said good-by to Joan she tried to control herself. She had dried her eyes and she fought to achieve the smile and the soothing and agreeable tone which she always used to the baby. Mrs. Jones had Joan in her sitting room on the second floor, and Millie went in there, and Joan saw her enter and lifted both arms in an appeal to be taken up from the floor. Millie picked her up, pouring out upon her that meaningless flood of words which Joan always found so delightful, while Mrs. Jones watched the two unhappily.

After a moment Millie said:

"I'll not be here for her birthday party."

"You might like to come in that afternoon," Mrs. Jones suggested; but Millie shook her head, and the tears burst from her eyes.

"I left a dress for her on my bed," she explained. "I've been making it the last month."

"She shall wear it," Mrs. Jones assured her, unable to feel anything but pity for the little old woman, and fighting for strength to maintain her decision that Millie must go.

Joan was pounding at Millie's face with her small hands, and Millie for a moment forgot Mrs. Jones, turning her attention to the baby again. "Good-by," she said. Joan wrinkled her nose and screamed with delight, and as she slapped Millie's cheeks the tears splashed under her hands. "I'm sorry I'm going, Joan," Millie told the baby. And Joan crowed, and Millie turned to Mrs. Jones and said:

"Take her."

Mrs. Jones held out her arms to the baby, but Joan had played that game before, and she knew what was expected of her. She laughed gleefully, threw her arms around Millie's neck, and snuggled her face into the nurse's shoulder; and Millie gave a little gasping cry and turned abruptly and set Joan down upon the floor and fled from the room. Only in the doorway she paused for a moment to turn and look back and to say over and over:

"I'm so sorry, Joan. I'm so sorry.

Millie's so sorry. Good-by, Joan. Good-by."

She stood there a moment longer, drenched in tears; and Joan, sobered by this spectacle, stared at her in perplexity and waved a small hand in a doubtful way.

"Yes, yes," Millie gasped. "Yes, Joan! Bye bye!"

So she waved an answering hand; then turned and fled, blind and stumbling, toward where the taxi waited at the door.

A waiting room is a fearful place. Millie had had some experience of waiting rooms and she dreaded them. She had been sitting in this particular waiting room at the employment agency for three days; a little woman, thin and taut, and just now curiously tremulous. Her eyes, inflamed and weary, looked blankly straight before her. And sometimes, for no apparent reason, they became suffused with tears; not merely misted with moisture, but drowned in a swimming, drenching flood which flowed over her lids and down her dry cheeks until she remembered to wipe away these evidences of the grief which racked her.

On the third day she found herself replying in a dull voice to the questions put to her by a woman who introduced herself by a name which Millie scarcely heard. She was not interested in the names of her mistresses; she had had so many of them. This woman's name might have been Brown or Jones. It happened to be Mrs. Smith.

Mrs. Smith asked question upon question, but Millie asked only one.

"Is the baby a boy or a girl?"

"A little girl," Mrs. Smith replied. And Millie's ravaged face seemed to lighten faintly at the word.

"I like little girls best," she confessed.

They arranged for Millie to come next morning; and Millie was for the rest of that day a little more cheerful. Her aching grief found anodyne in the prospect of having another baby to love.

Horsie

WHEN young Mrs. Gerald Cruger came home from the hospital, Miss Wilmarth came along with her and the baby. Miss Wilmarth was an admirable trained nurse, sure and calm and tireless, with a real taste for the arranging of flowers in bowls and vases. She had never known a patient to receive so many flowers, or such uncommon ones; yellow violets and strange lilies and little white orchids poised like a bevy of delicate moths along green branches. Care and thought must have been put into their selection that they, like all the other fragile and costly things she kept about her, should be so right for young Mrs. Cruger. No one who knew her could have caught up the telephone and lightly bidden the florist to deliver her one of his five-dollar assortments of tulips, stock, and daffodils. Camilla Cruger was no complement to garden blooms.

Reprinted from *The Portable Dorothy Parker*, Brendan Gill, ed., revised & enlarged edition (New York: Viking, 1960), pp. 129–154. First published in *After Such Pleasures* (1933). Copyright 1932, © 1960 by Dorothy Parker. Reprinted by permission of Viking Penguin Inc.

Sometimes, when she opened the shiny boxes and carefully grouped the cards, there would come a curious expression upon Miss Wilmarth's face. Playing over shorter features, it might almost have been one of wistfulness. Upon Miss Wilmarth, it served to perfect the strange resemblance that she bore through her years; her face was truly complete with that look of friendly melancholy peculiar to the gentle horse. It was not, of course, Miss Wilmarth's fault that she looked like a horse. Indeed, there was nowhere to attach any blame. But the resemblance remained.

She was tall, pronounced of bone, and erect of carriage; it was somehow impossible to speculate upon her appearance undressed. Her long face was innocent, indeed ignorant, of cosmetics, and its color stayed steady. Confusion, heat, or haste caused her neck to flush crimson. Her mild hair was pinned with loops of nicked black wire into a narrow knot, practical to support her little high cap, like a charlotte russe from a bake-shop. She had big, trustworthy hands, scrubbed and dry, with nails cut short and so deeply cleaned with some small sharp instrument that the ends stood away from the spatulate finger-tips. Gerald Cruger, who nightly sat opposite her at his own dinner table, tried not to see her hands. It irritated him to be reminded by their sight that they must feel like straw matting and smell of white soap. For him, women who were not softly lovely were simply not women.

He tried, too, so far as it was possible to his beautiful manners, to keep his eyes from her face. Not that it was unpleasant—a kind face, certainly. But, as he told Camilla, once he looked he stayed fascinated, awaiting the toss and the whinny.

"I love horses, myself," he said to Camilla, who lay all white and languid on her apricot satin chaise-longue. "I'm a fool for a horse. Ah, what a noble animal, darling! All I say is, nobody has any business to go around looking like a horse and behaving as if it were all right. You don't catch horses going around looking like people, do you?"

He did not dislike Miss Wilmarth; he only resented her. He had no bad wish in the world for her, but he waited with longing the day she would leave. She was so skilled and rhythmic in her work that she disrupted the household but little. Nevertheless, her presence was an onus. There was that thing of dining with her every evening. It was a chore for him, certainly, and one that did not ease with repetition, but there was no choice. Everyone had always heard of trained nurses' bristling insistence that they be not treated as servants; Miss Wilmarth could not be asked to dine with the maids. He would not have dinner out; be away from *Camilla?* It was too much to expect the maids to institute a second dinner service or to carry trays, other than Camilla's, up and down the stairs. There were only three servants and they had work enough.

"Those children," Camilla's mother was wont to say, chuckling. "Those two kids. The independence of them! Struggling along on cheese and kisses. Why, they hardly let me pay for the trained nurse. And it was all we could do, last Christmas, to make Camilla take the Packard and the chauffeur."

So Gerald dined each night with Miss Wilmarth. The small dread of his hour with her struck suddenly at him in the afternoon. He would forget it for stretches of minutes, only to be smitten sharper as the time drew near. On his way home from his office, he found grim entertainment in rehearsing his table talk, and plotting desperate innovations to it.

Cruger's Compulsory Conversations: Lesson I, a Dinner with a Miss Wilmarth, a Trained Nurse. Good evening, Miss Wilmarth. Well! And how were the patients all day? That's good, that's fine. Well! The baby gained two ounces, did she? That's fine. Yes, that's right, she will be before we know it. That's right. Well! Mrs. Cruger seems to be getting stronger every day, doesn't she? That's good, that's fine. That's right, up and about before we know it. Yes, she certainly will. Well! Any visitors today? That's good. Didn't stay too long, did they? That's fine. Well! No, no, no, Miss Wilmarth—*you* go ahead. I wasn't going to say anything at all, really. No, really. Well! Well! I see where they found those two aviators after all. Yes, they certainly do run risks. That's right. Yes. Well! I see where they've been having a regular old-fashioned blizzard out west. Yes, we certainly have had a mild winter. That's right. Well! I see where they held up that jeweler's shop right in broad daylight on Fifth Avenue. Yes, I certainly don't know what we're coming to. That's right. Well! I see the cat. Do you see the cat? The cat is on the mat. It certainly is. Well! Pardon me, Miss Wilmarth, but must you look so much like a horse? Do you like to look like a horse, Miss Wilmarth? That's good, Miss Wilmarth, that's fine. You certainly do, Miss Wilmarth. That's right. Well! Will you for God's sake finish your oats, Miss Wilmarth, and let me get out of this?

Every evening he reached the dining-room before Miss Wilmarth and stared gloomily at silver and candle-flame until she was upon him. No sound of footfall heralded her coming, for her ample canvas oxfords were soled with rubber; there would be a protest of parquet, a trembling of ornaments, a creak, a rustle, and the authoritative smell of stiff linen; and there she would be, set for her ritual of evening cheer.

"Well, Mary," she would cry to the waitress, "you know what they say—better late than never!"

But no smile would mellow Mary's lips, no light her eyes. Mary, in converse with the cook, habitually referred to Miss Wilmarth as "that one." She wished no truck with Miss Wilmarth or any of the others of her guild; always in and out of a person's pantry.

Once or twice Gerald saw a strange expression upon Miss Wilmarth's face as she witnessed the failure of her adage with the maid. He could not quite classify it. Though he did not know, it was the look she sometimes had when she opened the shiny white boxes and lifted the exquisite, scentless blossoms that were sent to Camilla. Anyway, whatever it was, it increased her equine resemblance to such a point that he thought of proffering her an apple.

But she always had her big smile turned toward him when she sat down. Then she would look at the thick watch strapped to her wrist and give a little squeal that brought the edges of his teeth together.

"Mercy!" she would say. "My good mercy! Why, I had no more idea it was so late. Well, you mustn't blame me, Mr. Cruger. Don't you scold *me*. You'll just have to blame that daughter of yours. She's the one that keeps us all busy."

"She certainly is," he would say. "That's right."

He would think, and with small pleasure, of the infant Diane, pink and undistinguished and angry, among the ruffles and *choux* of her bassinet. It was her doing that Camilla had stayed so long away from him in the odorous limbo of the hospital, her doing that Camilla lay all day upon her apricot satin chaise-longue. "We must take our time," the doctor said, "just ta-a-ake our ti-yem." Yes; well, that would all be because of young Diane. It was because of her, indeed, that night upon night he must face Miss Wilmarth and comb up conversation. All right, young Diane, there you are and nothing to do about it. But you'll be an only child, young woman, that's what you'll be.

Always Miss Wilmarth followed her opening pleasantry about the baby with a companion piece. Gerald had come to know it so well he could have said it in duet with her.

"You wait," she would say. "Just you wait. You're the one that's going to be kept busy when the beaux start coming around. You'll see. That young lady's going to be a heart-breaker if ever I saw one."

"I guess that's right," Gerald would say, and he would essay a small laugh and fail at it. It made him uncomfortable, somehow embarrassed him to hear Miss Wilmarth

17

banter of swains and conquest. It was unseemly, as rouge would have been unseemly on her long mouth and perfume on her flat bosom.

He would hurry her over to her own ground. "Well!" he would say. "Well! And how were the patients all day?"

But that, even with the baby's weight and the list of the day's visitors, seldom lasted past the soup.

"Doesn't that woman ever go out?" he asked Camilla. "Doesn't our Horsie ever rate a night off?"

"Where would she want to go?" Camilla said. Her low, lazy words had always the trick of seeming a little weary of their subject.

"Well," Gerald said, "she might take herself a moonlight canter around the park."

"Oh, she doubtless gets a thrill out of dining with you," Camilla said. "You're a man, they tell me, and she can't have seen many. Poor old horse. She's not a bad soul."

"Yes," he said. "And what a round of pleasure it is, having dinner every night with Not a Bad Soul."

"What makes you think," Camilla said, "that I am caught up in any whirl of gaiety, lying here?"

"Oh, darling," he said. "Oh, my poor darling. I didn't mean it, honestly I didn't. Oh, *Lord*, I didn't mean it. How could I complain, after all you've been through,

and I haven't done a thing? Please, sweet, please. Ah,
Camilla, say you know I didn't mean it."

"After all," Camilla said, "you just have her at dinner.
I have her around all day."

"Sweetheart, please," he said. "Oh, poor angel."

He dropped to his knees by the chaise-longue and
crushed her limp, fragrant hand against his mouth. Then
he remembered about being very, very gentle. He ran
little apologetic kisses up and down her fingers and murmured of gardenias and lilies and thus exhausted his
knowledge of white flowers.

Her visitors said that Camilla looked lovelier than
ever, but they were mistaken. She was only as lovely as
she had always been. They spoke in hushed voices of the
new look in her eyes since her motherhood; but it was
the same far brightness that had always lain there. They
said how white she was and how lifted above other people; they forgot that she had always been pale as moonlight and had always worn a delicate disdain, as light as
the lace that covered her breast. Her doctor cautioned
tenderly against hurry, besought her to take recovery
slowly—Camilla, who had never done anything quickly
in her life. Her friends gathered, adoring, about the apricot satin chaise-longue where Camilla lay and moved
her hands as if they hung heavy from her wrists; they
had been wont before to gather and adore at the white

satin sofa in the drawing-room where Camilla reclined, her hands like heavy lilies in a languid breeze. Every night, when Gerald crossed the threshold of her fragrant room, his heart leaped and his words caught in his throat; but those things had always befallen him at the sight of her. Motherhood had not brought perfection to Camilla's loveliness. She had had that before.

Gerald came home early enough, each evening, to have a while with her before dinner. He made his cocktails in her room, and watched her as she slowly drank one. Miss Wilmarth was in and out, touching flowers, patting pillows. Sometimes she brought Diane in on display, and those would be minutes of real discomfort for Gerald. He could not bear to watch her with the baby in her arms, so acute was his vicarious embarrassment at her behavior. She would bring her long head down close to Diane's tiny, stern face and toss it back again high on her rangy neck, all the while that strange words, in a strange high voice, came from her.

"Well, her wuzza booful dirl. Ess, her wuzza. Her wuzza, wuzza, wuzza. Ess, her *wuzz*." She would bring the baby over to him. "See, Daddy. Isn't us a gate, bid dirl? Isn't us booful? Say 'nigh-nigh,' Daddy. Us doe teepy-bye, now. Say 'nigh-nigh.'"

Oh, God.

Then she would bring the baby to Camilla. "Say

'nigh-nigh,' " she would cry. " 'Nigh-nigh,' Mummy."

"If that brat ever calls you 'Mummy,'" he told Camilla once, fiercely, "I'll turn her out in the snow."

Camilla would look at the baby, amusement in her slow glance. "Good night, useless," she would say. She would hold out a finger, for Diane's pink hand to curl around. And Gerald's heart would quicken, and his eyes sting and shine.

Once he tore his gaze from Camilla to look at Miss Wilmarth, surprised by the sudden cessation of her falsetto. She was no longer lowering her head and tossing it back. She was standing quite still, looking at him over the baby; she looked away quickly, but not before he had seen that curious expression on her face again. It puzzled him, made him vaguely uneasy. That night, she made no further exhortations to Diane's parents to utter the phrase "nigh-nigh." In silence she carried the baby out of the room and back to the nursery.

One evening, Gerald brought two men home with him; lean, easily dressed young men, good at golf and squash rackets, his companions through his college and in his clubs. They had cocktails in Camilla's room, grouped about the chaise-longue. Miss Wilmarth, standing in the nursery adjoining, testing the temperature of the baby's milk against her wrist, could hear them all talking lightly and swiftly, tossing their sentences into the air to hang there unfinished. Now and again she could distinguish Camilla's lazy voice; the others stopped immediately when she spoke, and when she was done there were long peals of laughter. Miss Wilmarth pictured her lying there, in golden chiffon and deep lace, her light figure turned always a little away from those about her, so that she must move her head and speak her slow words over her shoulder to them. The trained nurse's face was astoundingly equine as she looked at the wall that separated them.

They stayed in Camilla's room a long time, and there was always more laughter. The door from the nursery into the hall was open, and presently she heard the door of Camilla's room being opened, too. She had been able to hear only voices before, but now she could distinguish Gerald's words as he called back from the threshold; they had no meaning to her.

"Only wait, fellers," he said. "Wait till you see Seabiscuit."

He came to the nursery door. He held a cocktail shaker in one hand and a filled glass in the other.

"Oh, Miss Wilmarth," he said. "Oh, good evening, Miss Wilmarth. Why, I didn't know this door was open —I mean, I hope we haven't been disturbing you."

"Oh, not the least little bit," she said. "Goodness."

"Well!" he said. "I—we were wondering if you

wouldn't have a little cocktail. Won't you please?" He held out the glass to her.

"Mercy," she said, taking it. "Why, thank you ever so much. Thank you, Mr. Cruger."

"And, oh, Miss Wilmarth," he said, "would you tell Mary there'll be two more to dinner? And ask her not to have it before half an hour or so, will you? Would you mind?"

"Not the least little bit," she said. "Of course I will."

"Thank you," he said. "Well! Thank you, Miss Wilmarth. Well! See you at dinner."

"Thank *you*," she said. "I'm the one that ought to thank *you*. For the lovely little cockytail."

"Oh," he said, and failed at an easy laugh. He went back into Camilla's room and closed the door behind him.

Miss Wilmarth set her cocktail upon a table, and went down to inform Mary of the impending guests. She felt light and quick, and she told Mary gaily, awaiting a flash of gaiety in response. But Mary received the news impassively, made a grunt but no words, and slammed out through the swinging doors into the kitchen. Miss Wilmarth stood looking after her. Somehow servants never seemed to — She should have become used to it.

Even though the dinner hour was delayed, Miss Wilmarth was a little late. The three young men were standing in the dining-room, talking all at once and laughing all together. They stopped their noise when Miss Wilmarth entered, and Gerald moved forward to perform introductions. He looked at her, and then looked away. Prickling embarrassment tormented him. He introduced the young men, with his eyes away from her.

Miss Wilmarth had dressed for dinner. She had discarded her linen uniform and put on a frock of dark blue taffeta, cut down to a point at the neck and given sleeves that left bare the angles of her elbows. Small, stiff ruffles occurred about the hips, and the skirt was short for its year. It revealed that Miss Wilmarth had clothed her ankles in roughened gray silk and her feet in black, casket-shaped slippers, upon which little bows quivered as if in lonely terror at the expanse before them. She had been busied with her hair; it was crimped and loosened, and ends that had escaped the tongs were already sliding from their pins. All the length of her nose and chin was heavily powdered; not with a perfumed dust, tinted to praise her skin, but with coarse, bright white talcum.

Gerald presented his guests; Miss Wilmarth, Mr. Minot; Miss Wilmarth, Mr. Forster. One of the young men, it turned out, was Freddy, and one, Tommy. Miss Wilmarth said she was pleased to meet each of them. Each of them asked her how she did.

She sat down at the candle-lit table with the three beautiful young men. Her usual evening vivacity was gone from her. In silence she unfolded her napkin and took up her soup spoon. Her neck glowed crimson, and her face, even with its powder, looked more than ever as if it should have been resting over the top rail of a paddock fence.

"Well!" Gerald said.

"Well!" Mr. Minot said.

"Getting much warmer out, isn't it?" Mr. Forster said. "Notice it?"

"It is, at that," Gerald said. "Well. We're about due for warm weather."

"Yes, we ought to expect it now," Mr. Minot said. "Any day now."

"Oh, it'll be here," Mr. Forster said. "It'll come."

"I love spring," said Miss Wilmarth. "I just love it."

Gerald looked deep into his soup plate. The two young men looked at her.

"Darn good time of year," Mr. Minot said. "Certainly is."

"And how it is!" Mr. Forster said.

They ate their soup.

There was champagne all through dinner. Miss Wilmarth watched Mary fill her glass, none too full. The wine looked gay and pretty. She looked about the table before she took her first sip. She remembered Camilla's voice and the men's laughter.

"Well," she cried. "Here's a health, everybody!"

The guests looked at her. Gerald reached for his glass and gazed at it as intently as if he beheld a champagne goblet for the first time. They all murmured and drank.

"Well!" Mr. Minot said. "Your patients seem to be getting along pretty well, Miss Witmark. Don't they?"

"I should say they do," she said. "And they're pretty nice patients, too. Aren't they, Mr. Cruger?"

"They certainly are," Gerald said. "That's right."

"They certainly are," Mr. Minot said. "That's what they are. Well. You must meet all sorts of people in your work, I suppose. Must be pretty interesting."

"Oh, sometimes it is," Miss Wilmarth said. "It depends on the people." Her words fell from her lips clear and separate, sterile as if each had been freshly swabbed with boracic acid solution. In her ears rang Camilla's light, insolent drawl.

"That's right," Mr. Forster said. "Everything depends on the people, doesn't it? Always does, wherever you go. No matter what you do. Still, it must be wonderfully interesting work. Wonderfully."

"Wonderful the way this country's come right up in

medicine," Mr. Minot said. "They tell me we have the greatest doctors in the world, right here. As good as any in Europe. Or Harley Street."

"I see," Gerald said, "where they think they've found a new cure for spinal meningitis."

"*Have* they really?" Mr. Minot said.

"Yes, I saw that, too," Mr. Forster said. "Wonderful thing. Wonderfully interesting."

"Oh, say, Gerald," Mr. Minot said, and he went from there into an account, hole by hole, of his most recent performance at golf. Gerald and Mr. Forster listened and questioned him.

The three young men left the topic of golf and came back to it again, and left it and came back. In the intervals, they related to Miss Wilmarth various brief items that had caught their eyes in the newspapers. Miss Wilmarth answered in exclamations, and turned her big smile readily to each of them. There was no laughter during dinner.

It was a short meal, as courses went. After it, Miss Wilmarth bade the guests good-night and received their bows and their "*Good* night, Miss Witmark." She said she was awfully glad to have met them. They murmured.

"Well, good night, then, Mr. Cruger," she said. "See you tomorrow!"

"Good night, Miss Wilmarth," Gerald said.

The three young men went and sat with Camilla. Miss Wilmarth could hear their voices and their laughter as she hung up her dark blue taffeta dress.

Miss Wilmarth stayed with the Crugers for five weeks. Camilla was pronounced well—so well that she could have dined downstairs on the last few nights of Miss Wilmarth's stay, had she been able to support the fardel of dinner at the table with the trained nurse.

"I really couldn't dine opposite that face," she told Gerald. "You go amuse Horsie at dinner, stupid. You must be good at it, by now."

"All right, I will, darling," he said. "But God keep me, when she asks for another lump of sugar, from holding it out to her on my palm."

"Only two more nights," Camilla said, "and then Thursday Nana'll be here, and she'll be gone forever."

"'Forever,' sweet, is my favorite word in the language," Gerald said.

Nana was the round and competent Scottish woman who had nursed Camilla through her childhood and was scheduled to engineer the unknowing Diane through hers. She was a comfortable woman, easy to have in the house; a servant, and knew it.

Only two more nights. Gerald went down to dinner whistling a good old tune.

"The old gray mare, she ain't what she used to be,
Ain't what she used to be, ain't what she used to be——"

The final dinners with Miss Wilmarth were like all
the others. He arrived first, and stared at the candles until
she came.

"Well, Mary," she cried on her entrance, "you know
what they say—better late than never."

Mary, to the last, remained unamused.

Gerald was elated all the day of Miss Wilmarth's de-
parture. He had a holiday feeling, a last-day-of-school
jubilation with none of its faint regret. He left his office
early, stopped at a florist's shop, and went home to Camilla.

Nana was installed in the nursery, but Miss Wilmarth
had not yet left. She was in Camilla's room, and he saw
her for the second time out of uniform. She wore a long
brown coat and a brown rubbed velvet hat of no definite shape. Obviously, she was in the middle of the em-
barrassments of farewell. The melancholy of her face
made it so like a horse's that the hat above it was pre-
posterous.

"Why, there's Mr. Cruger!" she cried.

"Oh, good evening, Miss Wilmarth," he said. "Well!
Ah, hello, darling. How are you, sweet? Like these?"

He laid a florist's box in Camilla's lap. In it were

strange little yellow roses, with stems and leaves and tiny, soft thorns all of blood red. Miss Wilmarth gave a little squeal at the sight of them.

"Oh, the darlings!" she cried. "Oh, the boo-fuls!"

"And these are for you, Miss Wilmarth," he said. He made himself face her and hold out to her a square, smaller box.

"Why, Mr. Cruger," she said. "For me, really? Why, really, Mr. Cruger."

She opened the box and found four gardenias, with green foil and pale green ribbon holding them together.

"Oh, now, really, Mr. Cruger," she said. "Why, I never in all my life—Oh, now, you shouldn't have done it. Really, you shouldn't. My good mercy! Well, I never saw anything so lovely in all my life. Did you, Mrs. Cruger? They're *lovely*. Well, I just don't know how to *begin* to thank you. Why, I just—well, I just adore them."

Gerald made sounds designed to convey the intelligence that he was glad she liked them, that it was nothing, that she was welcome. Her squeaks of thanks made red rise back of his ears.

"They're nice ones," Camilla said. "Put them on, Miss Wilmarth. And these are awfully cunning, Jerry. Sometimes you have your points."

"Oh, I didn't think I'd *wear* them," Miss Wilmarth

said. "I thought I'd just take them in the box like this, so they'd keep better. And it's such a nice box—I'd like to have it. I—I'd like to keep it."

She looked down at the flowers. Gerald was in sudden horror that she might bring her head down close to them and toss it back high, crying "wuzza, wuzza, wuzza" at them the while.

"Honestly," she said, "I just can't take my eyes *off* them."

"The woman is mad," Camilla said. "It's the effect of living with us, I suppose. I hope we haven't ruined you for life, Miss Wilmarth."

"Why, Mrs. Cruger," Miss Wilmarth cried. "Now, really! I was just telling Mrs. Cruger, Mr. Cruger, that I've never been on a pleasanter case. I've just had the time of my life, all the time I was here. I don't know when I—honestly, I can't stop looking at my posies, they're so lovely. Well, I just can't thank you for all you've done."

"Well, we ought to thank you, Miss Wilmarth," Gerald said. "We certainly ought."

"I really hate to say 'good-by,'" Miss Wilmarth said. "I just hate it."

"Oh, don't say it," Camilla said. "I never dream of saying it. And remember, you must come in and see the baby, any time you can."

"Yes, you certainly must," Gerald said. "That's right."

"Oh, I will," Miss Wilmarth said. "Mercy, I just don't dare go take another look at her, or I wouldn't be able to leave, ever. Well, what am I thinking of! Why, the car's been waiting all this time. Mrs. Cruger simply insists on sending me home in the car, Mr. Cruger. Isn't she terrible?"

"Why, not at all," he said. "Why, of course."

"Well, it's only five blocks down and over to Lexington," she said, "or I really couldn't think of troubling you."

"Why, not at all," Gerald said. "Well! Is that where you live, Miss Wilmarth?"

She lived in some place of her own sometimes? She wasn't always disarranging somebody else's household?

"Yes," Miss Wilmarth said. "I have Mother there."

Oh. Now Gerald had never thought of her having a mother. Then there must have been a father, too, some time. And Miss Wilmarth existed because two people once had loved and known. It was not a thought to dwell upon.

"My aunt's with us, too," Miss Wilmarth said. "It makes it nice for Mother—you see, Mother doesn't get around very well any more. It's a little bit crowded for the three of us—I sleep on the davenport when I'm home, between cases. But it's so nice for Mother, having my aunt there."

Even in her leisure, then, Miss Wilmarth was a disruption and a crowd. Never dwelling in a room that had been planned only for her occupancy; no bed, no corner of her own; dressing before other people's mirrors, touching other people's silver, never looking out one window that was hers. Well. Doubtless she had known nothing else for so long that she did not mind or even ponder.

"Oh, yes," Gerald said. "Yes, it certainly must be fine for your mother. Well! Well! May I close your bags for you, Miss Wilmarth?"

"Oh, that's all done," she said. "The suitcase is downstairs. I'll just go get my hat-box. Well, good-by, then, Mrs. Cruger, and take care of yourself. And thank you a thousand times."

"Good luck, Miss Wilmarth," Camilla said. "Come see the baby."

Miss Wilmarth looked at Camilla and at Gerald standing beside her, touching one long white hand. She left the room to fetch her hat-box.

"I'll take it down for you, Miss Wilmarth," Gerald called after her.

He bent and kissed Camilla gently, very, very gently.

"Well, it's nearly over, darling," he said. "Sometimes I am practically convinced that there is a God."

"It was darn decent of you to bring her gardenias," Camilla said. "What made you think of it?"

"I was so crazed at the idea that she was really going," he said, "that I must have lost my head. No one was more surprised than I, buying gardenias for Horsie. Thank the Lord she didn't put them on. I couldn't have stood that sight."

"She's not really at her best in her street clothes," Camilla said. "She seems to lack a certain *chic*." She stretched her arms slowly above her head and let them sink slowly back. "That was a fascinating glimpse of her home life she gave us. Great fun."

"Oh, I don't suppose she minds," he said. "I'll go down now and back her into the car, and that'll finish it."

He bent again over Camilla.

"Oh, you look so lovely, sweet," he said. "So *lovely*."

Miss Wilmarth was coming down the hall, when Gerald left the room, managing a pasteboard hat-box, the florist's box, and a big leather purse that had known service. He took the boxes from her, against her protests, and followed her down the stairs and out to the motor at the curb. The chauffeur stood at the open door. Gerald was glad of that presence.

"Well, good luck, Miss Wilmarth," he said. "And thank you so much."

"Thank *you*, Mr. Cruger," she said. "I—I can't tell you how I've enjoyed it all the time I was here. I never had a pleasanter— And the flowers, and everything. I just don't know what to say. I'm the one that ought to thank *you*."

She held out her hand, in a brown cotton glove. Anyway, worn cotton was easier to the touch than dry, corded flesh. It was the last moment of her. He scarcely minded looking at the long face on the red, red neck.

"Well!" he said. "Well! Got everything? Well, good luck, again, Miss Wilmarth, and don't forget us."

"Oh, I won't," she said. "I—oh, I won't do that."

She turned from him and got quickly into the car, to sit upright against the pale gray cushions. The chauffeur placed her hat-box at her feet and the florist's box on the seat beside her, closed the door smartly, and returned to his wheel. Gerald waved cheerily as the car slid away. Miss Wilmarth did not wave to him.

When she looked back, through the little rear window, he had already disappeared in the house. He must have run across the sidewalk—run, to get back to the fragrant room and the little yellow roses and Camilla. Their little pink baby would lie sleeping in its bed. They would be alone together; they would dine alone together

by candlelight; they would be alone together in the
night. Every morning and every evening Gerald would
drop to his knees beside her to kiss her perfumed hand
and call her sweet. Always she would be perfect, in
scented chiffon and deep lace. There would be lean, easy
young men, to listen to her drawl and give her their
laughter. Every day there would be shiny white boxes
for her, filled with curious blooms. It was perhaps fortunate that no one looked in the limousine. A beholder
must have been startled to learn that a human face could
look as much like that of a weary mare as did Miss Wilmarth's.

Presently the car swerved, in a turn of the traffic. The
florist's box slipped against Miss Wilmarth's knee. She
looked down at it. Then she took it on her lap, raised
the lid a little and peeped at the waxy white bouquet. It
would have been all fair then for a chance spectator;
Miss Wilmarth's strange resemblance was not apparent,
as she looked at her flowers. They were her flowers. A
man had given them to her. She had been given flowers.
They might not fade maybe for days. And she could
keep the box.

BRING! BRING!

I.

MISS ROOKER dreamed that she was on board the *Falcon* in Marblehead Harbor. Dr. Fish was uncorking a bottle of champagne, contorting his face grotesquely, his gray mustache pushed up so that it seemed to envelop his red nose. Dr. Harrington, tall and thin in his white flannels, stood beside the gramophone, singing with wide open mouth, his eyes comically upturned towards the low cabin ceiling: his white flannel arm was round Miss Paine's waist. As he sang he seemed to draw her tighter and tighter against his side, his face darkened, Miss Paine began to scream. The cork came out with a loud pop, froth poured onto the napkin. Miss Rooker held out her glass to be filled, and a great blob of champagne froth fell upon the front of her skirt. It was her white duck skirt which buttoned all the way down with large mother-of-pearl buttons. "Oh—Dr. Harrington!" she cried. Dr. Fish reached down a hand to wipe it away—she was transfixed with delight and horror when instead he unbuttoned one of the buttons, at the same time bringing his mustached face very close to hers and intensely smiling. She had no clothes on, and he was touching her knee. Dr. Harrington sang louder, Miss Paine screamed

11

Reprinted from *Bring! Bring! and Other Stories* (New York: Boni & Liveright, 1925), pp. 11–36

louder, the gramophone cawed and squealed, and now
Dr. Fish was uncorking one bottle after another—
pop! pop! pop! She sat in the stern of the tender,
trailing one hand in the water of the dark harbor, as
they rowed rapidly away from the yacht. Dr. Harrington, slightly drunk, was driving rather recklessly
—from side to side of the Boulevard went the car, and
Miss Rooker and Dr. Fish were tumbled together: he
pinched her side. She would be late—they would be
late—long after midnight. The sky was already growing light. Birds began singing. A sparrow, rather
large, ridiculously large, opened his mouth wide and
started shouting in through her window: "Bring!
Bring! Bring! Bring! Bring! . . ." She woke at
this. A sparrow was chirping noisily in the wild cherry
tree outside her window. She was in Duxbury. It
was a hot morning in summer. She was "on a case"
—Mrs. Oldkirk. Mrs. Oldkirk would be waking and
would want her glass of hot milk. Perhaps Mrs. Oldkirk had been calling? She listened. No. Nothing
but the sparrows and the crickets. But it was time to
get up. Why on earth should she be dreaming, after
all this time, of Dr. Harrington and Dr. Fish? Five
years ago. Possibly because Mr. Oldkirk reminded
her of Dr. Fish. . . . Brushing her black hair before
the mirror, and looking into her dark-pupilled brown
eyes, she felt melancholy. She was looking very well
—very pretty. She sang softly, so as not to disturb
Mrs. Oldkirk in the next room: *"And when I told
—them—how beautiful you were—they wouldn't be—*

lieve—me; they wouldn't be—lieve—me." Delicious, a deep cold bath on a sultry morning like this: and to-day the bathing would be good, a high tide about twelve o'clock. Mr. Oldkirk and Miss Lavery would be going in. . . . Miss Lavery was Mrs. Oldkirk's cousin. . . . Well, it really was disgraceful, the way they behaved! Pretending to "keep house" for Mrs. Oldkirk! Did anybody else notice it? And Mr. Oldkirk was very nice looking, she liked his sharp blue eyes, humorous. *"And—when—I—told—them—how beautiful you were—"*

Mrs. Oldkirk was already awake, her hands clasped under her braided hair, her bare white elbows tilted upward.

"Good morning, Miss Rooker," she said languidly.

"Good morning, Mrs. Oldkirk. Did you sleep well?"

"No, it was too hot . . . far too hot . . . even without a sheet. The ice melted in the lemonade. It was disgusting."

"Will you want your hot milk this morning?"

"Oh, yes—certainly. What time is it, Miss Rooker?"

"Just seven-thirty."

All the windows in the house were open, as Miss Rooker passed through the hall and down the stairs. The sea-wind sang softly through the screens, sea-smells and pine-smells, and the hot morning was like a cage full of birds. "Bring! Bring!" the sparrow had shouted—remarkable dream—and here she was, bringing, bringing hot milk on a hot morning, bringing hot milk to a lazy neurotic woman (rather pretty) who was no more an invalid than she was herself. Why did she want to stay in bed? Why did she want a nurse? A slave would have done as well—there wasn't the slightest occasion for medical knowledge. The massage, of course. But it was very queer. There was something wrong. And Miss Lavery and Mr. Oldkirk were always talking together till past midnight, talking, talking!

Hilda was lighting the fire in the kitchen range, her pale face saturated with sleep, her pale hair untidy. The green shades were still down over the windows, and the kitchen had the air of an aquarium, the oak floor scrubbed white as bone.

"Good morning, Hilda—how was the dance last night?"

"Lovely. . . . But oh, sweet hour, how sleepy I am!"

"You look it. You'll lose your beauty."

"Oh, go on!"

The fire began crackling in the range: small slow curls of blue smoke oozed out round the stove lids. Miss Rooker went to the ice-chest, took out the bottle of milk. Holding it by the neck, she returned upstairs. On the way she saw Mary setting the breakfast table: she, too, looked pale and sleepy, had been to the dance. *"And when I told—them—"* She poured the creamy milk into the aluminum saucepan and lit the alcohol lamp. Then she went to the window and watched the sea-gulls circling over the naked hot

mud flats. Seals sat in rows. On the beach, fringed
with eel-grass, near at hand, Mr. Oldkirk's green dory
was pulled far up, and rested amid gray matted seaweed.

By the time she had given Mrs. Oldkirk her hot milk,
bathed the patient's face and hands and wrists (beautiful wrists, languid and delicate) with cold water,
and combed her hair, breakfast was half over . . .
Mr. Oldkirk, leaning forward on one elbow, was regarding Miss Lavery with a look humorous and intent.
Iced grapefruit.

"Ah, here's Miss Rooker," said Mr. Oldkirk, glancing up at her quizzically, and pulling back her chair
with outstretched hand. . . . "Good morning, Miss
Rooker. Sit down. We have a problem for you to
solve."

Miss Lavery was wearing her pale green satin morning gown. It was becoming to her—oh, quite dis-
gustingly—set off, somehow her long, blue eyes, lazy
and liquid, tilted up at the corners a little like a China-
man's. But far too negligee. The idea of coming
down to breakfast like that—with Mr. Oldkirk!

"I'm no good at riddles. Ask me an easy one."

"Oh, this is extremely simple," Mr. Oldkirk said,
with just a hint of malice, "merely a question of observation—observation of one's self."

Miss Lavery thought this was very funny—she gave
a snort of laughter, and stifled it behind her napkin.
Really! thought Miss Rooker—when she leaned for-

ward like that!—with that low, loose morning gown!
Scandalous.

"You're good at observing, Miss Rooker—tell us,
how long does a love affair last—a normal, you know,
ordinary one, I mean?"

"Well, upon my soul!" cried Miss Rooker. "Is *that*
what's worrying you?"

"Oh, yes, poor man, he's terribly worried about it."
Miss Lavery snickered, eying Mr. Oldkirk with a
gleaming mock derision. "He's been wrangling with
me, all breakfast through, about it."

"Seriously, Miss Rooker—" he pretended to ignore
Miss Lavery—"it's an important scientific question.
And of course a charming young lady like you has
had *some* experience of—er—the kind?"

Miss Rooker blushed. She was annoyed, she could
not have said exactly why. She was annoyed with both
of them: just slightly. Glancing at Mr. Oldkirk (yes,
he certainly looked like Dr. Fish) she said shortly:

"You want to know too much."

Mr. Oldkirk opened his eyes. "Oh!" he said—then
again, in a lower tone, "Oh." He frowned at his plate,
breathed densely through his grayish mustache. . . .
Then, to Miss Lavery, who had suddenly become rather
frigid, and was looking at Miss Rooker just a little
impudently:

"Any more coffee, Helen? . . ."

"Not a drop."

"Damn." He got up, slow and tall.

"Berty! You shouldn't swear before Miss Rooker."

Miss Lavery's words tinkled as coldly and sharply as ice in a pitcher of lemonade. Hateful woman! Were they trying to make her feel like a servant?

"Oh, I'm quite used to it, Miss Lavery. Doctors, you know!"

Miss Lavery, leaning plump, bare elbows on the mahogany table, clasping long, white fingers lightly before her chin, examined Miss Rooker attentively. "Oh, yes, you're used to doctors, of course. They're very immoral, aren't they?"

Miss Rooker turned scarlet, gulped her coffee, while Miss Lavery just perceptibly smiled.

"How's the patient this morning?" Mr. Oldkirk turned around from the long window, where he had been looking out at the bay. "Any change?"

"No. She's the picture of health, as she *always* is." Miss Rooker was downright. "I think she ought to be up."

"That's not my opinion, Miss Rooker, nor the doctor's either."

"Well—"

"She's been ordered a long rest."

"A rest, do you call it! With—" Miss Rooker broke off, angry and helpless.

"With what?" Mr. Oldkirk's tone was inquisitively sharp.

"Oh, well," Miss Rooker sighed, "I don't understand these nervous cases: I suppose I don't. If *I* had *my* way, though, I'd have her up and out before you could say Jack Robinson."

Mr. Oldkirk was dry and decisive.

"That's your opinion, Miss Rooker. You would probably admit that Dr. Hedgley knows a little more about it than you do."

He sauntered out of the dining room, hands in pockets, lazy and powerful.

"Another slice of toast, Miss Rooker? . . ." Miss Lavery asked the question sweetly, touching with one finger the electric toaster. . . .

"No, thank you, Miss Lavery. Not any more."

II.

"Don't read, Miss Rooker, it's too hot, I can't listen. And I'm so tired of all those he saids and she saids and said he with a wicked smile! It's a tiresome story. Talk to me instead. And bring me a glass of lemonade."

Mrs. Oldkirk turned on her side and smiled lazily. Indolent gray eyes.

"It *is* hot."

"I suppose you enjoy nursing, Miss Rooker?"

"Oh, yes, it has its ups and downs. Like everything else."

"You get good pay, and massaging keeps your hands soft. You must see lots of interesting things, too."

"Very. You see some very queer things, sometimes. Queer cases. Living as one of the family; you know, in all sorts of out-of-the-way places—"

"I suppose *my* case seems queer to you." Mrs. Oldkirk's eyes were still and candid, profound.

"Well—it does—a little! , . ."

The two women looked at each other, smiling. The brass traveling clock struck eleven. Mary could be heard sweeping the floor in Miss Rooker's room: *swish, swish.*

"It's not so queer when you know about it." She turned her head away, somber.

"No, nothing is, I suppose. Things are only queer seen from the outside."

"Ah, you're unusually wise for a young girl, Miss Rooker! I daresay you've had lots of experience."

Miss Rooker blushed, flattered.

"Do you know a good deal about men?"

"Well—I don't know—it all depends what you mean."

Mrs. Oldkirk yawned, throwing her head back on the pillow. She folded her hands beneath her head, and smiled curiously at the ceiling.

"I mean what damned scoundrels they are . . . though I guess there are a *few* exceptions. . . . You'd better go for your swim, if you're going. . . . Bring me some hot milk at twelve-thirty. . . . No lunch. . . . And I think I'll sit on the balcony for an hour at three. You can ask them to join me there for tea. Iced tea."

"You'd better try a nap."

"Nap! Not much. Bring me that rotten book. I'll read a little."

Miss Rooker, going into her room for the towel, met Mary coming out: a dark sensual face. "Oh, you dancing girl!" she murmured, and Mary giggled. The hot sea-wind sang through the screen, salt-smelling. She threw the towel over her shoulder and stood for a moment at the window, melancholy, looking past the railed end of the balcony, and over the roof of the veranda. The cherries in the wild cherry tree were dark red and black, nearly ripe. The bay itself looked hot—the lazy small waves flashed hotly and brilliantly, a wide lazy glare of light all the way from the monument hill to the outer beach, of which the white dunes seemed positively to be burning up. Marblehead was better, the sea was colder there, rocks were better than all this horrible mud—the nights were cooler : and there was more life in the harbor. The good old *Falcon!* "Them was happy days"—that was what Dr. Fish was always saying. And Mr. Oldkirk was extraordinarily like him, the same lazy vigorous way of moving about, slow heavy limbs, a kind of slothful grace. She heard his voice. He and Miss Lavery were coming out, the screen door banged, they emerged bare-headed into the heat, going down the shell path to the bathhouse. "Hell infernal," he was saying, opening one hand under the sunlight as one might do to feel a rain—"which reminds me of the girl whose name was Helen Fernald . . . that's what you are: hell infernal." Miss Lavery opened her pongee parasol, and her words were lost under it. She was very graceful—provocatively graceful, and her gait had about it a light inviting freedom, something virginal and at the same time sensuous. She gave a sudden screech of laughter as they went round the corner of the bathhouse.

"It's not a nursing case at all," she thought, standing before her mirror—"they pay me to amuse her, that's all—or *she* pays me—which is it?" She leaned close to the mirror, regarding her white almost transparent-seeming temples, the full red mouth (she disliked her lower lip, which she had always thought too heavy—pendulous) and the really beautiful dark hair, parted, and turned away from her brow in heavy wings. *"And when I told them—"* Did Mr. Oldkirk like her eyes? That awful word—oh, really dreadful, but so true—Dr. Fish had used about her eyes! But Mr. Oldkirk seemed to like Chinese eyes better. . . . Ought she to stay—just being a kind of lady's maid like this? And it wasn't right. No: it wasn't decent. She would like to say so to their faces. "I think you'd better get another nurse at the end of the week, Mr. Oldkirk—I don't approve of the way things are going on here—no, I don't approve at all. Shameful, that's what it is!—you and Miss Lavery—" But what did she know about him and Miss Lavery? . . . A pang. Misery. They were just cousins. A filthy mind she had, imagining such things. She had heard them talking, talking on the veranda, they went out late at night in the green dory: once, three nights ago, she had thought she heard soft footsteps in the upstairs hall, and a murmur, a long sleepy murmur. . . . *"How beautiful you wer-r-r-r-re."*

The bathhouse was frightfully hot—like an oven.

It smelt of salt wood and seaweed. She took her clothes off slowly, feeling sand on the boards under her feet. She could hear Miss Lavery moving in the next "cell," occasionally brushing her clothes against the partition or thumping an elbow. Helen Lavery. Probably about thirty—maybe twenty-eight. A social service worker, they said—she'd be a fine social service worker! Going round and pretending to be a fashionable lady. Sly, tricky, disgusting creature! . . . And a one-piece bathing suit, with no stockings! She was too clever to miss any chance like that. Of course, she had a beautiful figure, though her legs were just a shade too heavy. And she used it for all it was worth.

Miss Lavery was already thigh-deep in the water (in the gap between two beds of eel-grass) wading, with a swaying slow grace, towards Mr. Oldkirk, who floated on his back with hardly more than his nose and mustache visible. She skimmed the water with swallow-swift hands, forward and back, as she plunged deeper. "Oo! delicious," she cried, and sank with a soft turmoil, beginning to swim. "Don't bump me," Mr. Oldkirk answered, blowing, "I'm taking a nap."

The sunlight beat like cymbals on the radiant beach. The green dory was almost too hot to touch, but Miss Rooker dragged and pushed it into the water, threw in the anchor, and shoved off. "Look out!" she sang, whacking a blade on the water.

"Hello! Where are you off to, Miss Rooker?" Mr. Oldkirk blew like a seal.

"Marblehead."

"Dangerous place for young ladies, Miss Rooker. Better not stay after dark!"

"Oh, Marblehead's an open book to me!" Miss Rooker was arch.

"Oh, it is, is it!" He gave a loud "Ha!" in the water, blowing bubbles. "Better take me, then!"

He took three vigorous strokes, reached up a black-haired hand to the gunwale, and hauling himself up, deliberately overturned the dory. Miss Rooker screamed, plunged sidelong past Mr. Oldkirk's head (saw him grinning) into the delicious cold shock of water. Down she went, and opening her eyes saw Mr. Oldkirk's green legs and blue body, wavering within reach—she took hold of his cold, hard knee, then flung her arms round his waist, hugged him ecstatically, pulled him under. They became, for a second, deliciously entangled under the water. The top of his head butted her knee, his hand slid across her hip. Then they separated, kicking each other, and rose, both sputtering.

"Trying—woof—to drown me?" he barked, shaking his head from side to side. "A nice trick!"

"*You* did it!" . . . Miss Rooker laughed, excited. She swam on her back, out of breath, looking at Mr. Oldkirk intensely. Had he guessed that there, under the water, she had touched him deliberately? There was something in his eyes—a small sharp gleam as of secret intimacy, a something admitted between them —or was it simply a question? . . . Averting his eyes,

suddenly, he swam to the upturned dory, and began
pushing it towards the shore. Miss Lavery, who
could not swim well, stood in shallow water, up to
her middle, breathlessly ducking up and down. She
looked rather ridiculous.

"What *are* you children doing!" she cried, chatter-
ing. "I'm cold; I think I'll go in."

Mr. Oldkirk pushed, swimming, thrashing the water
with powerful legs. "You ought to be"—he puffed—
"damned glad"—he puffed—"to be cold on a day like
this"—he puffed—"Helen!" Then he called: "Come
on—Miss Rooker! Give me a hand. Too heavy."

She put her hands against one corner of the green
bow. The dory moved slowly. It would be easy to
touch his legs again—the thought pleased her, she
laughed, and, letting her laughing mouth sink below
the surface, blew a wild froth of bubbles. Their faces
were very close to one another. Miss Lavery, standing
and watching, lifted conscious elbows to tuck her hair
under her bathing cap.

"You swim like a fish," said Mr. Oldkirk. "Must
be a granddaughter of Venus. Was it Venus who
came up out of Duxbury Bay on a good-sized clam-
shell?"

Miss Rooker laughed, puzzled. Was he flattering,
or being sarcastic? . . . What about Venus? . . .
"No," she said. "Nothing like that. But, oh, how
I do enjoy it!"

In shallow water they righted and emptied the dory,
restored the oars. While Mr. Oldkirk, getting into

the boat, began hauling himself out to the anchor, which had fallen in, Miss Rooker climbed the beach toward the bathhouse. Miss Lavery stood before the door, taking off her bathing cap. Her face was hard. She was shivering. She struck her cap against the door jamb, sharply, and gave a little malicious smile.

"I know why you did that!" she said. She stepped in and shut the door.

Miss Rooker stared at the door, furious. Her first impulse was to open the door and shout something savagely injurious. The vixen! the snake! . . . She went into her own room—hot as an oven—and dropped the bathing suit off. Miss Lavery had suspected something. . . . Well, let her suspect. . . . She dried herself slowly with the warm towel, enjoying the beauty of her cool body. Let her suspect! Good for her. . . . Ah, it *had* been delicious! . . . She would let Miss Lavery hear her singing. *"And—when—I—told—them—"* . . .

Five minutes later Miss Lavery banged her door and departed, and Miss Rooker smiled.

III.

Mrs. Oldkirk, languid and pretty in her pink crepe-de-chine dressing gown, leaned back in her wicker chair resting her head on the tiny pillow and closed her eyes. Her silver-embroidered slippers, with blue pompoms, were crossed on the foot stool. The magazine had fallen from her hand. "Oh, how heavenly," she

murmured. "Nothing as heavenly as a scalp massage.
. . . You're very skilful, Miss Rooker. You have
the touch. . . . Not so much on the top, now—a little
more at the sides, and down the neck. . . ."

Miss Rooker, standing behind the wicker chair,
stared over her patient's head into the dressing-table
mirror. Massage. Massage. It was insufferably hot.
The breeze had dropped. She felt drowsy. Zeek—
zeek—zeek—zeek—zeek sang the crickets in the hot
grass under the afternoon sun. The long seething trill
of a cicada died languidly away—in a tree, she supposed. She remembered seeing a locust attacked by
a huge striped bee—or was it a wasp? They had
fallen together to the ground, in the dry grass, and
the heavy bee, on top, curving its tail malevolently,
stung the gray-pleated upturned belly, the poor creature shrilling and spinning all the while. Then the
bee—or wasp—had zoomed away, and the gray locust,
color of ashes, spun on its back a little and lay still.
. . . Down the smooth soft neck. A curved pressure
over and behind the ears. What was the matter with
Mrs. Oldkirk? Too young for change of life—no.
Something mysterious. She was very pretty, in her
soft lazy supercilious way, and had a queer rich indif-
ferent-seeming personality. A loose screw somewhere
—too bad. Or was it that she was—Mrs. Oldkirk
yawned.

"I love to feel someone fooling about my head:
the height of luxury. When I go to the hairdresser I
feel like staying all day. I'd like to pay them to keep

on for hours. Especially if it's a man! Something
thrilling about having your hair done by a man. Don't
you know—? It tickles you all over."

Miss Rooker laughed, embarrassed. Singular re-
mark! "Yes—" she answered slowly, as if with un-
certainty. "I think I know what you mean."

"I'm sure you do—you haven't those naughty black
eyes for nothing, Miss Rooker! Ha, ha!"

"Oh, well, I suppose I'm human." Miss Rooker
snickered. *Were* her eyes "naughty"? She wanted to
study them in the glass, but was afraid that Mrs.
Oldkirk would be watching. Zeek—zeek—zeek—zeek
—sang the crickets. What were they doing, where
were they now? Was Miss Lavery taking a nap?
Were they out in the car? . . . Her arms were beginning to be tired.

"Tell me, Miss Rooker, as woman to woman—what
do you think of men?" Mrs. Oldkirk opened her gray
eyes, lazily smiling.

"Well—I like them very much, if that's what you
mean."

"*I* suppose so! You're still young. How old are
you, if you don't mind my asking?"

"Twenty-four."

"Ah, yes. Very young. Lucky girl. . . . But you
wait fourteen years! *Then* see what you think of
men."

"Do they seem so different?"

"They don't seem, my dear girl, they *are*. It's when
you're young that they *seem*. Later on, you begin to

understand them—you get their number. And then—oh, my God—you want to exterminate the whole race of them. The nasty things!"

Miss Rooker felt herself blushing.

"Oh, I'm sure they aren't as bad as all that!"

"Devil's advocate! Miss Rooker. . . . Don't try to defend them. . . . They're all rotten. . . . Oh, I don't mean that there isn't a dear old parson here and there, you know—but then you remember the words of the song—'Even staid old country preachers are engaging tango teachers.' You can't get away from it! . . . No, the man doesn't live that I'd trust with a lead nickel. . . . By which, however, I don't mean that I don't enjoy having my hair done by a man! Ha, ha!" . . . Mrs. Oldkirk gave a queer little laugh, flaccid and bitter. She looked at herself, with parted lips, in the mirror: a distant sort of scrutiny, slightly contemptuous. Then, relaxing, she added: "Take my advice—don't ever marry. It's a snare and a delusion."

"Why, I should *love* to marry!"

"Oh, you would! . . . In that case all I can say is I hope you'll have better luck than *I* did. . . ."

Miss Rooker was silent, confused.

"Tell me, has Berty, my husband—been flirting with you? Don't be afraid to be frank—it doesn't matter, you know!"

"Why, no—he hasn't."

"You probably wouldn't tell me if he had. But if he hasn't yet he will. . . . Give him time!"

"Good heavens! What a thing to say!"

"Do I shock you? . . . I know him like the alphabet! . . . poor old satyr."

"You seem to!"

"Ah, I do. . . . Absolutely no principles—not a principle. There's only one thing in Berty I've never been able to understand; and that's his dislike of Miss Lavery. Ha, ha! That's why I have Miss Lavery keep house for me."

Mrs. Oldkirk closed her eyes again, faintly smiling. To say such things to her, a stranger! What was the matter with her? Miss Rooker was appalled at the indiscretion. . . . And Mr. Oldkirk and Miss Lavery going out in the dory at midnight, and talking, talking, long after everyone else had gone to bed. . . . And that footstep in the hall, and the long affectionate murmur—surely Miss Lavery's voice? . . . It was all extraordinary. She had never been in such a queer place. She thought of the incident in the water, and then of Miss Lavery banging her rubber cap against the door, and saying, "I know why you did that!" . . . Well, Mrs. Oldkirk could sneer at Berty all she liked; but for *her* part—

"I think that's enough, thank you, Miss Rooker. . . . You didn't forget about the iced tea, did you?"

"No."

"Do you know where Mr. Oldkirk and Miss Lavery are?"

"No—I think Miss Lavery's lying down."

"Well—three-thirty. . . . Would you mind picking up my magazine? It's fallen down. . . ."

. . . Miss Rooker descended the shell path and sauntered along the hot beach. She sank down on the dry bedded seaweed in the shadow of the bluff. The seaweed was still warm, and smelt strongly of the sea . . . zeek—zeek—zeek—zeek. . . . So her eyes were naughty, were they! Perhaps they had more effect than she knew. She smiled. Perhaps Mr. Oldkirk— her heart was beating violently, she opened her book, for a delicious moment the type swam beneath her eyes.

IV.

"Good-night," said Miss Rooker. As she switched off the light, and shut the door the brass traveling clock began striking ten. She went down the stairs, carrying the tray. The lamp on the sitting-room table was lighted, a book was open, there was a smell of cigarette smoke, but nobody was there. The warm wind sang through the screens, fluttered the pages of the book. Where were they? She felt depressed. It was horrible—horrible! She wouldn't stand it— not another day. Not another hour. . . . "Mr. Oldkirk, I want to speak to you: I feel that I can't stay on here. . . ." Would he try to persuade her to stay? Ah! perhaps he wouldn't. . . . They were probably on the beach—not on the veranda, anyway, or she would hear them. She carried the tray into the kitchen, pushing open the swing door. Mary and Hilda were standing close together at one of the windows looking out into the night. Hilda was giggling. They were watching something, standing still and tense.

"He is—he is—" said Mary in a low excited voice—"he's kissing her. You can see their heads go together."

"Well, what do you know." Hilda's drawl was full of wonder. "Sweet hour! . . . I wouldn't mind it much myself."

"Look! Do you see?"

Miss Rooker let go of the swing door: it shut with a thump, and the two girls started. Hilda's face was scarlet, Mary was saturnine.

"Who's kissing who?" asked Miss Rooker, looking angrily from one to the other. Hilda, still blushing, and putting back a strand of pale hair from her moist forehead, answered, embarrassed:

"It's Mr. Oldkirk and Miss Lavery, miss."

"Oh! And do you think it's nice to be spying on them?"

"We weren't spying—if they do it right on the beach, in the bright moonlight, it's *their* lookout."

Miss Rooker put down the tray and walked back to the sitting room. Her temples were throbbing. What ought she to do? It was disgraceful—before the servants like this! Shameful. She would do something —she *must*. She went out to the veranda, banging the screen door very loudly. Perhaps they would hear it, though she half hoped they wouldn't. She went down the path, and as she got to the beach, with its moonlit

seaweed, she began whistling, and walking towards
the dory. What was she going to say? She didn't
know. Something. Something short and angry. The
moonlight showed them quite clearly—they must have
heard her coming, for Mr. Oldkirk was striking a
match and lighting a cigarette, and they had moved
apart. They were sitting against the dory.

"Why, it's Miss Rooker!" cried Mr. Oldkirk. "Come
and bask in the moonlight, Miss Rooker."

She looked down at them, feeling her lips very
dry.

"I felt I ought to tell you that the servants are
watching you," she said. There was a silence—dreadful. Then, as Mr. Oldkirk said, "Oh!" and began
scrambling to his feet, she turned and walked away.
. . . That would teach them! That would give that
hateful woman something to think about!

In the sitting room she sat down by the table, sank
her forehead in her hands and pretended to be reading.
What was going to happen? The screen door banged
and Miss Lavery stood in the hall, under the light.

"Miss Rooker," she said. Her voice shook a little.
Miss Rooker rose and moved slowly toward her, a
little pleased to observe the whiteness of her face.

"What is it?"

"You're a dirty spy," was the low answer, and Miss
Lavery, turning, went calmly up the stairs. She could
think of nothing to say—nothing! . . . She burned.
Anyone would suppose it was *she* who was in the
wrong! . . . She sat down again, holding the book

on her knee. . . . She would like to kill that woman!
. . . Where was Mr. Oldkirk? She must see Mr.
Oldkirk and tell him to his face—she would say that
she was leaving tomorrow. Yes—tomorrow! By the
nine-fifteen. They would have to get another nurse.
Horrible! She discovered that she was trembling.
What was she trembling for? She was angry, that
was all, angry and excited—she wasn't afraid. Afraid
of what? Mr. Oldkirk? Absurd! . . . She began
reading. The words seemed large, cold and meaningless, the sentences miles apart. "Said she, he said, and
said she, smiling cruelly." Zeek—zeek—zeek—zeek—
zeek—those damned crickets! Where, where in God's
name was Mr. Oldkirk? . . . Should she saunter out
and meet him on the beach? No. He would put two
and two together. He would remember her touching
him in the water. She must wait—pretend to be
reading. "The blind man put out his white, extraordinarily sensitive hand, his hand that was conscious
as . . . eyes are conscious. He touched her face, and
she shrank. His forefinger felt for the scar along
the left side of her jaw and ran lightly, it seemed
almost hysterically, over it—with hysterical joy.
'Marie!' he cried—'it's little Marie! . . .'" How perfectly ridiculous. . . . And to think of Mrs. Oldkirk,
all the time thinking that Berty disliked Miss Lavery!
That was the limit. Yes, the absolute limit. "That's
why I have her keep house for me." But did she,
perhaps, know it all the time? . . . Ah! . . . She

was sly, Mrs. Oldkirk! . . . It was possible—it was perfectly possible. . . . Extraordinary house!

She heard footsteps on the veranda. She sprang up, switched off the light, leaving the sitting room in comparative darkness. She'd meet him in the hall—She took two steps, and then, as the door slammed, stopped. No. She saw him standing, tall and indolent, just inside the door. He peered, wrinkling his forehead, in her direction, apparently not seeing her.

"Miss Rooker—are you there?"

"Yes."

He came into the dark room, and she took an uncertain step towards him. He stopped, they faced each other, and there was a pause. He stood against the lighted doorway, huge and silhouetted.

"I wanted to speak to you"—his voice was embarrassed and gentle—"and I wanted to wait till Miss Lavery had gone to bed."

"Oh."

"Yes. . . . I wanted to apologize to you. It must have been very distressing for you."

"Oh, not at all, I assure you. . . . Not in the least." Her voice was a little faint—she put her hand against the edge of the table.

"I'm sure it was. Please forgive me. . . . Miss Lavery, you know—" He gave a queer uneasy laugh, as if there was something he wanted to say but couldn't. What was it—was it that Miss Lavery was the one? She felt, suddenly, extraordinarily happy.

"I think I'd better leave tomorrow," she answered then, looking away. "I think it would be better."

"Nonsense, my dear Miss Rooker! Don't think of it. . . . Why should you?"

Her heart was beating so violently that she could hardly think. She heard him breathing heavily and quickly.

"Well," she said, "I think it would be better."

"Why? There's no earthly reason. . . . No." As she made no reply, he went on—"It won't happen again —I can promise you *that!*" He again laughed, but this time as if he were thinking of something else, thinking of something funny that was going to happen. . . . Was he laughing at Miss Lavery?

Miss Rooker, unsteady, took a step to pass him, but he put out his hand. It closed upon her wrist. With his other hand he took slow possession of hers. She drew back, but only a little.

"Please," she said.

"Please what?"

"Let me go."

"Only when you've given me a promise."

"What?"

"That you'll stay here—with *me.*"

"Oh—you know I can't!"

She was trembling, and was ashamed to know that his hands must feel her trembling.

"Promise!" he said. She looked up at him—his eyes were wide, dark, beautiful, full of intention.

"Very well, I promise."

"Good! Good girl. . . ." He did not let go of her hand and wrist. "I'll make it up to you. . . . Don't mind Miss Lavery!"

"You *are* dreadful!" She gave a laugh, her self-possession coming back to her.

"*Am* I?" He beamed. "Well, I am, sometimes! . . . But what about you?"

"Oh, I'm awful!" she answered. She drew away her hand, rather slowly, reluctantly. "Good-night, then."

"Good-night."

She turned on the landing to look down at him. He smiled, his humorous eyes twinkling, and she smiled in return. . . . Heavens! how extraordinary, how simply extraordinary, how perfectly extraordinary. . . . She stared at her reflection in the glass. "Naughty" eyes? No—they were beautiful. She had never looked so beautiful—never. . . . Perhaps he would knock at her door? She locked it. . . . She combed her hair, and as she did so, began humming, "*And—when—I—told—them—*" Then she remembered Mrs. Oldkirk in the next room, and stopped. Poor old thing! . . . She got into bed and lay still, smiling. The wind whispered in the screen, the crickets were singing louder than ever. They liked a hot night like this. Zeek—zeek. Mr. Oldkirk passed along the hall. . . . Ah, the nice tall man with nice eyes, the very, very nice man! . . .

ELLEN GLASGOW

THE SHADOWY THIRD

WHEN the call came I remember that I turned
from the telephone in a romantic flutter. Though I
had spoken only once to the great surgeon, Roland
Maradick, I felt on that December afternoon that
to speak to him only once—to watch him in the
operating-room for a single hour—was an adventure which drained the colour and the excitement
from the rest of life. After all these years of work
on typhoid and pneumonia cases, I can still feel the
delicious tremor of my young pulses; I can still see
the winter sunshine slanting through the hospital
windows over the white uniforms of the nurses.

"He didn't mention me by name. Can there
be a mistake?" I stood, incredulous yet ecstatic,
before the superintendent of the hospital.

"No, there isn't a mistake. I was talking to
him before you came down." Miss Hemphill's
strong face softened while she looked at me. She
was a big, resolute woman, a distant Canadian
relative of my mother's, and the kind of nurse
I had discovered in the month since I had come
up from Richmond, that Northern hospital boards,
if not Northern patients, appear instinctively to

3

Reprinted from *The Shadowy Third* (Garden City, NY: Doubleday, Page & Co.,
1923), pp. 3–43. First published in slightly different form in *Scribner's* (1916)

select. From the first, in spite of her hardness, she had taken a liking—I hesitate to use the word "fancy" for a preference so impersonal—to her Virginia cousin. After all, it isn't every Southern nurse, just out of training, who can boast a kinswoman in the superintendent of a New York hospital.

"And he made you understand positively that he meant me?" The thing was so wonderful that I simply couldn't believe it.

"He asked particularly for the nurse who was with Miss Hudson last week when he operated. I think he didn't even remember that you had a name. When I asked if he meant Miss Randolph, he repeated that he wanted the nurse who had been with Miss Hudson. She was small, he said, and cheerful-looking. This, of course, might apply to one or two of the others, but none of these was with Miss Hudson."

"Then I suppose it is really true?" My pulses were tingling. "And I am to be there at six o'clock?"

"Not a minute later. The day nurse goes off duty at that hour, and Mrs. Maradick is never left by herself for an instant."

"It is her mind, isn't it? And that makes it all the stranger that he should select me, for I have had so few mental cases."

"So few cases of any kind," Miss Hemphill was

4

smiling, and when she smiled I wondered if the other nurses would know her. "By the time you have gone through the treadmill in New York, Margaret, you will have lost a good many things besides your inexperience. I wonder how long you will keep your sympathy and your imagination? After all, wouldn't you have made a better novelist than a nurse?"

"I can't help putting myself into my cases. I suppose one ought not to?"

"It isn't a question of what one ought to do, but of what one must. When you are drained of every bit of sympathy and enthusiasm, and have got nothing in return for it, not even thanks, you will understand why I try to keep you from wasting yourself."

"But surely in a case like this—for Doctor Maradick?"

"Oh, well, of course—for Doctor Maradick." She must have seen that I implored her confidence, for, after a minute, she let fall carelessly a gleam of light on the situation: "It is a very sad case when you think what a charming man and a great surgeon Doctor Maradick is."

Above the starched collar of my uniform I felt the blood leap in bounds to my cheeks. "I have spoken to him only once," I murmured, "but he is charming, and so kind and handsome, isn't he?"

5

THE SHADOWY THIRD

"His patients adore him."

"Oh, yes, I've seen that. Everyone hangs on his visits." Like the patients and the other nurses, I also had come by delightful, if imperceptible, degrees to hang on the daily visits of Doctor Maradick. He was, I suppose, born to be a hero to women. From my first day in his hospital, from the moment when I watched, through closed shutters, while he stepped out of his car, I have never doubted that he was assigned to the great part in the play. If I had been ignorant of his spell—of the charm he exercised over his hospital—I should have felt it in the waiting hush, like a drawn breath, which followed his ring at the door and preceded his imperious footstep on the stairs. My first impression of him, even after the terrible events of the next year, records a memory that is both careless and splendid. At that moment, when, gazing through the chinks in the shutters, I watched him, in his coat of dark fur, cross the pavement over the pale streaks of sunshine, I knew beyond any doubt—I knew with a sort of infallible prescience—that my fate was irretrievably bound up with his in the future. I knew this, I repeat, though Miss Hemphill would still insist that my foreknowledge was merely a sentimental gleaning from indiscriminate novels. But it wasn't only first love, impressionable as my kinswoman believed me to be. It wasn't only the

6

way he looked. Even more than his appearance—more than the shining dark of his eyes, the silvery brown of his hair, the dusky glow in his face—even more than his charm and his magnificence, I think, the beauty and sympathy in his voice won my heart. It was a voice, I heard someone say afterwards, that ought always to speak poetry.

So you will see why—if you do not understand at the beginning, I can never hope to make you believe impossible things!—so you will see why I accepted the call when it came as an imperative summons. I couldn't have stayed away after he sent for me. However much I may have tried not to go, I know that in the end I must have gone. In those days, while I was still hoping to write novels, I used to talk a great deal about "destiny" (I have learned since then how silly all such talk is), and I suppose it was my "destiny" to be caught in the web of Roland Maradick's personality. But I am not the first nurse to grow love-sick about a doctor who never gave her a thought.

"I am glad you got the call, Margaret. It may mean a great deal to you. Only try not to be too emotional." I remember that Miss Hemphill was holding a bit of rose-geranium in her hand while she spoke—one of the patients had given it to her from a pot she kept in her room, and the scent of the flower is still in my nostrils—or my memory. Since then—oh, long since then

7

—I have wondered if she also had been caught in the web.

"I wish I knew more about the case." I was pressing for light. "Have you ever seen Mrs. Maradick?"

"Oh, dear, yes. They have been married only a little over a year, and in the beginning she used to come sometimes to the hospital and wait outside while the doctor made his visits. She was a very sweet-looking woman then—not exactly pretty, but fair and slight, with the loveliest smile, I think, I have ever seen. In those first months she was so much in love that we used to laugh about it among ourselves. To see her face light up when the doctor came out of the hospital and crossed the pavement to his car, was as good as a play. We never tired of watching her—I wasn't superintendent then, so I had more time to look out of the window while I was on day duty. Once or twice she brought her little girl in to see one of the patients. The child was so much like her that you would have known them anywhere for mother and daughter."

I had heard that Mrs. Maradick was a widow, with one child, when she first met the doctor, and I asked now, still seeking an illumination I had not found, "There was a great deal of money, wasn't there?"

"A great fortune. If she hadn't been so at-

8

tractive, people would have said, I suppose, that Doctor Maradick married her for her money. Only," she appeared to make an effort of memory, "I believe I've heard somehow that it was all left in trust away from Mrs. Maradick if she married again. I can't, to save my life, remember just how it was; but it was a queer will, I know, and Mrs. Maradick wasn't to come into the money unless the child didn't live to grow up. The pity of it——"

A young nurse came into the office to ask for something—the keys, I think, of the operating-room, and Miss Hemphill broke off inconclusively as she hurried out of the door. I was sorry that she left off just when she did. Poor Mrs. Maradick! Perhaps I was too emotional, but even before I saw her I had begun to feel her pathos and her strangeness.

My preparations took only a few minutes. In those days I always kept a suitcase packed and ready for sudden calls; and it was not yet six o'clock when I turned from Tenth Street into Fifth Avenue, and stopped for a minute, before ascending the steps, to look at the house in which Doctor Maradick lived. A fine rain was falling, and I remember thinking, as I turned the corner, how depressing the weather must be for Mrs. Maradick. It was an old house, with damp-looking walls (though that may have been because of the rain)

9

and a spindle-shaped iron railing which ran up
the stone steps to the black door, where I noticed
a dim flicker through the old-fashioned fanlight.
Afterwards I discovered that Mrs. Maradick had
been born in the house—her maiden name was
Calloran—and that she had never wanted to live
anywhere else. She was a woman—this I found
out when I knew her better—of strong attachments
to both persons and places; and though Doctor
Maradick had tried to persuade her to move
uptown after her marriage, she had clung, against
his wishes, to the old house in lower Fifth Avenue.
I dare say she was obstinate about it in spite of
her gentleness and her passion for the doctor.
Those sweet, soft women, especially when they
have always been rich, are sometimes amazingly
obstinate. I have nursed so many of them since—
women with strong affections and weak intellects—
that I have come to recognize the type as soon as
I set eyes upon it.

My ring at the bell was answered after a little
delay, and when I entered the house I saw that the
hall was quite dark except for the waning glow
from an open fire which burned in the library.
When I gave my name, and added that I was the
night nurse, the servant appeared to think my
humble presence unworthy of illumination. He
was an old negro butler, inherited perhaps from
Mrs. Maradick's mother, who, I learned afterwards,

10

was from South Carolina; and while he passed me on his way up the staircase, I heard him vaguely muttering that he "wa'n't gwinter tu'n on dem lights twel de chile had done playin'."

To the right of the hall, the soft glow drew me into the library, and crossing the threshold timidly, I stooped to dry my wet coat by the fire. As I bent there, meaning to start up at the first sound of a footstep, I thought how cosy the room was after the damp walls outside to which some bared creepers were clinging; and I was watching the strange shapes and patterns the firelight made on the old Persian rug, when the lamps of a slowly turning motor flashed on me through the white shades at the window. Still dazzled by the glare, I looked round in the dimness and saw a child's ball of red and blue rubber roll towards me out of the gloom of the adjoining room. A moment later, while I made a vain attempt to capture the toy as it spun past me, a little girl darted airily, with peculiar lightness and grace, through the doorway, and stopped quickly, as if in surprise at the sight of a stranger. She was a small child—so small and slight that her footsteps made no sound on the polished floor of the threshold; and I remember thinking while I looked at her that she had the gravest and sweetest face I had ever seen. She couldn't— I decided this afterwards—have been more than six or seven years old, yet she stood there with a curious

11

prim dignity, like the dignity of an elderly person, and gazed up at me with enigmatical eyes. She was dressed in Scotch plaid, with a bit of red ribbon in her hair, which was cut in a fringe over her forehead and hung very straight to her shoulders. Charming as she was, from her uncurled brown hair to the white socks and black slippers on her little feet, I recall most vividly the singular look in her eyes, which appeared in the shifting light to be of an indeterminate colour. For the odd thing about this look was that it was not the look of childhood at all. It was the look of profound experience, of bitter knowledge.

"Have you come for your ball?" I asked; but while the friendly question was still on my lips, I heard the servant returning. In my confusion I made a second ineffectual grasp at the plaything, which had rolled away from me into the dusk of the drawing-room. Then, as I raised my head, I saw that the child also had slipped from the room; and without looking after her I followed the old negro into the pleasant study above, where the great surgeon awaited me.

Ten years ago, before hard nursing had taken so much out of me, I blushed very easily, and I was aware at the moment when I crossed Doctor Maradick's study that my cheeks were the colour of peonies. Of course, I was a fool—no one knows this better than I do—but I had never been alone,

12

even for an instant, with him before, and the man was more than a hero to me, he was—there isn't any reason now why I should blush over the confession—almost a god. At that age I was mad about the wonders of surgery, and Roland Maradick in the operating-room was magician enough to have turned an older and more sensible head than mine. Added to his great reputation and his marvelous skill, he was, I am sure of this, the most splendid-looking man, even at forty-five, that one could imagine. Had he been ungracious —had he been positively rude to me, I should still have adored him; but when he held out his hand, and greeted me in the charming way he had with women, I felt that I would have died for him. It is no wonder that a saying went about the hospital that every woman he operated on fell in love with him. As for the nurses—well, there wasn't a single one of them who had escaped his spell—not even Miss Hemphill, who could have been scarcely a day under fifty.

"I am glad you could come, Miss Randolph. You were with Miss Hudson last week when I operated?"

I bowed. To save my life I couldn't have spoken without blushing the redder.

"I noticed your bright face at the time. Brightness, I think, is what Mrs. Maradick needs. She finds her day nurse depressing." His eyes rested

13

so kindly upon me that I have suspected since that he was not entirely unaware of my worship. It was a small thing, heaven knows, to flatter his vanity—a nurse just out of a training-school— but to some men no tribute is too insignificant to give pleasure.

"You will do your best, I am sure." He hesitated an instant—just long enough for me to perceive the anxiety beneath the genial smile on his face—and then added gravely, "We wish to avoid, if possible, having to send her away."

I could only murmur in response, and after a few carefully chosen words about his wife's illness, he rang the bell and directed the maid to take me upstairs to my room. Not until I was ascending the stairs to the third storey did it occur to me that he had really told me nothing. I was as perplexed about the nature of Mrs. Maradick's malady as I had been when I entered the house.

I found my room pleasant enough. It had been arranged—at Doctor Maradick's request, I think—that I was to sleep in the house, and after my austere little bed at the hospital, I was agreeably surprised by the cheerful look of the apartment into which the maid led me. The walls were papered in roses, and there were curtains of flowered chintz at the window, which looked down on a small formal garden at the rear of the house. This the maid told me, for it was too dark for me

14

to distinguish more than a marble fountain and a fir-tree, which looked old, though I afterwards learned that it was replanted almost every season.

In ten minutes I had slipped into my uniform and was ready to go to my patient; but for some reason—to this day I have never found out what it was that turned her against me at the start— Mrs. Maradick refused to receive me. While I stood outside her door I heard the day nurse trying to persuade her to let me come in. It wasn't any use, however, and in the end I was obliged to go back to my room and wait until the poor lady got over her whim and consented to see me. That was long after dinner—it must have been nearer eleven than ten o'clock—and Miss Peterson was quite worn out by the time she came for me.

"I'm afraid you'll have a bad night," she said as we went downstairs together. That was her way, I soon saw, to expect the worst of everything and everybody.

"Does she often keep you up like this?"

"Oh, no, she is usually very considerate. I never knew a sweeter character. But she still has this hallucination——"

Here again, as in the scene with Doctor Maradick, I felt that the explanation had only deepened the mystery. Mrs. Maradick's hallucination, whatever form it assumed, was evidently a subject for evasion and subterfuge in the household. It

15

was on the tip of my tongue to ask, "What is her hallucination?"—but before I could get the words past my lips we had reached Mrs. Maradick's door, and Miss Peterson motioned me to be silent. As the door opened a little way to admit me, I saw that Mrs. Maradick was already in bed, and that the lights were out except for a night-lamp burning on a candle-stand beside a book and a carafe of water.

"I won't go in with you," said Miss Peterson in a whisper; and I was on the point of stepping over the threshold when I saw the little girl, in the dress of Scotch plaid, slip by me from the dusk of the room into the electric light of the hall. She held a doll in her arms, and as she went by she dropped a doll's work-basket in the doorway. Miss Peterson must have picked up the toy, for when I turned in a minute to look for it I found that it was gone. I remember thinking that it was late for a child to be up—she looked delicate, too—but, after all, it was no business of mine, and four years in a hospital had taught me never to meddle in things that do not concern me. There is nothing a nurse learns quicker than not to try to put the world to rights in a day.

When I crossed the floor to the chair by Mrs. Maradick's bed, she turned over on her side and looked at me with the sweetest and saddest smile.

"You are the night nurse," she said in a

16

gentle voice; and from the moment she spoke I knew that there was nothing hysterical or violent about her mania—or hallucination, as they called it. "They told me your name, but I have forgotten it."

"Randolph—Margaret Randolph." I liked her from the start, and I think she must have seen it.

"You look very young, Miss Randolph."

"I am twenty-two, but I suppose I don't look quite my age. People usually think I am younger."

For a minute she was silent, and while I settled myself in the chair by the bed, I thought how strikingly she resembled the little girl I had seen first in the afternoon, and then leaving her room a few moments before. They had the same small, heart-shaped faces, coloured ever so faintly; the same straight, soft hair, between brown and flaxen; and the same large, grave eyes, set very far apart under arched eyebrows. What surprised me most, however, was that they both looked at me with that enigmatical and vaguely wondering expression—only in Mrs. Maradick's face the vagueness seemed to change now and then to a definite fear— a flash, I had almost said, of startled horror.

I sat quite still in my chair, and until the time came for Mrs. Maradick to take her medicine not a word passed between us. Then, when I bent over her with the glass in my hand, she raised her

17

head from the pillow and said in a whisper of suppressed intensity:

"You look kind. I wonder if you could have seen my little girl?"

As I slipped my arm under the pillow I tried to smile cheerfully down on her. "Yes, I've seen her twice. I'd know her anywhere by her likeness to you."

A glow shone in her eyes, and I thought how pretty she must have been before illness took the life and animation out of her features. "Then I know you're good." Her voice was so strained and low that I could barely hear it. "If you weren't good you couldn't have seen her."

I thought this queer enough, but all I answered was, "She looked delicate to be sitting up so late."

A quiver passed over her thin features, and for a minute I thought she was going to burst into tears. As she had taken the medicine, I put the glass back on the candle-stand, and bending over the bed, smoothed the straight brown hair, which was as fine and soft as spun silk, back from her forehead. There was something about her—I don't know what it was—that made you love her as soon as she looked at you.

"She always had that light and airy way, though she was never sick a day in her life," she answered calmly after a pause. Then, groping for my hand, she whispered passionately, "You must not tell

18

him—you must not tell any one that you have seen her!"

"I must not tell any one?" Again I had the impression that had come to me first in Doctor Maradick's study, and afterwards with Miss Peterson on the staircase, that I was seeking a gleam of light in the midst of obscurity.

"Are you sure there isn't any one listening—that there isn't any one at the door?" she asked, pushing aside my arm and raising herself on the pillows.

"Quite, quite sure. They have put out the lights in the hall."

"And you will not tell him? Promise me that you will not tell him." The startled horror flashed from the vague wonder of her expression. "He doesn't like her to come back, because he killed her."

"Because he killed her!" Then it was that light burst on me in a blaze. So this was Mrs. Maradick's hallucination! She believed that her child was dead—the little girl I had seen with my own eyes leaving her room; and she believed that her husband—the great surgeon we worshipped in the hospital—had murdered her. No wonder they veiled the dreadful obsession in mystery! No wonder that even Miss Peterson had not dared to drag the horrid thing out into the light! It was the kind of hallucination one simply couldn't stand having to face.

19

"There is no use telling people things that nobody believes," she resumed slowly, still holding my hand in a grasp that would have hurt me if her fingers had not been so fragile. "Nobody believes that he killed her. Nobody believes that she comes back every day to the house. Nobody believes—and yet you saw her——"

"Yes, I saw her—but why should your husband have killed her?" I spoke soothingly, as one would speak to a person who was quite mad. Yet she was not mad, I could have sworn this while I looked at her.

For a moment she moaned inarticulately, as if the horror of her thoughts were too great to pass into speech. Then she flung out her thin, bare arm with a wild gesture.

"Because he never loved me!" she said. "He never loved me!"

"But he married you," I urged gently while I stroked her hair. "If he hadn't loved you, why should he have married you?"

"He wanted the money—my little girl's money. It all goes to him when I die."

"But he is rich himself. He must make a fortune from his profession."

"It isn't enough. He wanted millions." She had grown stern and tragic. "No, he never loved me. He loved someone else from the beginning—before I knew him."

20

THE SHADOWY THIRD

It was quite useless, I saw, to reason with her. If she wasn't mad, she was in a state of terror and despondency so black that it had almost crossed the border-line into madness. I thought once that I would go upstairs and bring the child down from her nursery; but, after a moment's hesitation, I realized that Miss Peterson and Doctor Maradick must have long ago tried all these measures. Clearly, there was nothing to do except soothe and quiet her as much as I could; and this I did until she dropped into a light sleep which lasted well into the morning.

By seven o'clock I was worn out—not from work but from the strain on my sympathy—and I was glad, indeed, when one of the maids came in to bring me an early cup of coffee. Mrs. Maradick was still sleeping—it was a mixture of bromide and chloral I had given her—and she did not wake until Miss Peterson came on duty an hour or two later. Then, when I went downstairs, I found the dining-room deserted except for the old housekeeper, who was looking over the silver. Doctor Maradick, she explained to me presently, had his breakfast served in the morning-room on the other side of the house.

"And the little girl? Does she take her meals in the nursery?"

She threw me a startled glance. Was it, I questioned afterwards, one of distrust or apprehension?

21

"There isn't any little girl. Haven't you heard?"

"Heard? No. Why, I saw her only yesterday."

The look she gave me—I was sure of it now—was full of alarm.

"The little girl—she was the sweetest child I ever saw—died just two months ago of pneumonia."

"But she couldn't have died." I was a fool to let this out, but the shock had completely unnerved me. "I tell you I saw her yesterday."

The alarm in her face deepened. "That is Mrs. Maradick's trouble. She believes that she still sees her."

"But don't you see her?" I drove the question home bluntly.

"No." She set her lips tightly. "I never see anything."

So I had been wrong, after all, and the explanation, when it came, only accentuated the terror. The child was dead—she had died of pneumonia two months ago—and yet I had seen her, with my own eyes, playing ball in the library; I had seen her slipping out of her mother's room, with her doll in her arms.

"Is there another child in the house? Could there be a child belonging to one of the servants?" A gleam had shot through the fog in which I was groping.

"No, there isn't any other. The doctors tried

22

bringing one once, but it threw the poor lady into such a state she almost died of it. Besides, there wouldn't be any other child as quiet and sweet-looking as Dorothea. To see her skipping along in her dress of Scotch plaid used to make me think of a fairy, though they say that fairies wear nothing but white or green."

"Has any one else seen her—the child, I mean —any of the servants?"

"Only old Gabriel, the coloured butler, who came with Mrs. Maradick's mother from South Carolina. I've heard that negroes often have a kind of second sight—though I don't know that that is just what you would call it. But they seem to believe in the supernatural by instinct, and Gabriel is so old and doty—he does no work except answer the door-bell and clean the silver— that nobody pays much attention to anything that he sees——"

"Is the child's nursery kept as it used to be?"

"Oh, no. The doctor had all the toys sent to the children's hospital. That was a great grief to Mrs. Maradick; but Doctor Brandon thought, and all the nurses agreed with him, that it was best for her not to be allowed to keep the room as it was when Dorothea was living."

"Dorothea? Was that the child's name?"

"Yes, it means the gift of God, doesn't it? She was named after the mother of Mrs. Mara-

23

dick's first husband, Mr. Ballard. He was the grave, quiet kind—not the least like the doctor."

I wondered if the other dreadful obsession of Mrs. Maradick's had drifted down through the nurses or the servants to the housekeeper; but she said nothing about it, and since she was, I suspected, a garrulous person, I thought it wiser to assume that the gossip had not reached her.

A little later, when breakfast was over and I had not yet gone upstairs to my room, I had my first interview with Doctor Brandon, the famous alienist who was in charge of the case. I had never seen him before, but from the first moment that I looked at him I took his measure almost by intuition. He was, I suppose, honest enough—I have always granted him that, bitterly as I have felt towards him. It wasn't his fault that he lacked red blood in his brain, or that he had formed the habit, from long association with abnormal phenomena, of regarding all life as a disease. He was the sort of physician—every nurse will understand what I mean—who deals instinctively with groups instead of with individuals. He was long and solemn and very round in the face; and I hadn't talked to him ten minutes before I knew he had been educated in Germany, and that he had learned over there to treat every emotion as a pathological manifestation. I used to wonder what he got out of life—what any one got out of

24

life who had analyzed away everything except the bare structure.

When I reached my room at last, I was so tired that I could barely remember either the questions Doctor Brandon had asked or the directions he had given me. I fell asleep, I know, almost as soon as my head touched the pillow; and the maid who came to inquire if I wanted luncheon decided to let me finish my nap. In the afternoon, when she returned with a cup of tea, she found me still heavy and drowsy. Though I was used to night nursing, I felt as if I had danced from sunset to daybreak. It was fortunate, I reflected, while I drank my tea, that every case didn't wear on one's sympathies as acutely as Mrs. Maradick's hallucination had worn on mine.

Through the day I did not see Doctor Maradick; but at seven o'clock when I came up from my early dinner on my way to take the place of Miss Peterson, who had kept on duty an hour later than usual, he met me in the hall and asked me to come into his study. I thought him handsomer than ever in his evening clothes, with a white flower in his buttonhole. He was going to some public dinner, the housekeeper told me, but, then, he was always going somewhere. I believe he didn't dine at home a single evening that winter.

"Did Mrs. Maradick have a good night?" He

25

had closed the door after us, and turning now with the question, he smiled kindly, as if he wished to put me at ease in the beginning.

"She slept very well after she took the medicine. I gave her that at eleven o'clock."

For a minute he regarded me silently, and I was aware that his personality—his charm—was focussed upon me. It was almost as if I stood in the centre of converging rays of light, so vivid was my impression of him.

"Did she allude in any way to her—to her hallucination?" he asked.

How the warning reached me—what invisible waves of sense-perception transmitted the message —I have never known; but while I stood there, facing the splendour of the doctor's presence, every intuition cautioned me that the time had come when I must take sides in the household. While I stayed there I must stand either with Mrs. Maradick or against her.

"She talked quite rationally," I replied after a moment.

"What did she say?"

"She told me how she was feeling, that she missed her child, and that she walked a little every day about her room."

His face changed—how I could not at first determine.

"Have you see Doctor Brandon?"

26

"He came this morning to give me his directions."

"He thought her less well to-day. He has advised me to send her to Rosedale."

I have never, even in secret, tried to account for Doctor Maradick. He may have been sincere. I tell only what I know—not what I believe or imagine—and the human is sometimes as inscrutable, as inexplicable, as the supernatural.

While he watched me I was conscious of an inner struggle, as if opposing angels warred somewhere in the depths of my being. When at last I made my decision, I was acting less from reason, I knew, than in obedience to the pressure of some secret current of thought. Heaven knows, even then, the man held me captive while I defied him.

"Doctor Maradick," I lifted my eyes for the first time frankly to his, "I believe that your wife is as sane as I am—or as you are."

He started. "Then she did not talk freely to you?"

"She may be mistaken, unstrung, piteously distressed in mind"—I brought this out with emphasis—"but she is not—I am willing to stake my future on it—a fit subject for an asylum. It would be foolish—it would be cruel to send her to Rosedale."

"Cruel, you say?" A troubled look crossed

27

his face, and his voice grew very gentle. "You do not imagine that I could be cruel to her?"

"No, I do not think that." My voice also had softened.

"We will let things go on as they are. Perhaps Doctor Brandon may have some other suggestion to make." He drew out his watch and compared it with the clock—nervously, I observed, as if his action were a screen for his discomfiture or perplexity. "I must be going now. We will speak of this again in the morning."

But in the morning we did not speak of it, and during the month that I nursed Mrs. Maradick I was not called again into her husband's study. When I met him in the hall or on the staircase, which was seldom, he was as charming as ever; yet, in spite of his courtesy, I had a persistent feeling that he had taken my measure on that evening, and that he had no further use for me.

As the days went by Mrs. Maradick seemed to grow stronger. Never, after our first night together, had she mentioned the child to me; never had she alluded by so much as a word to her dreadful charge against her husband. She was like any woman recovering from a great sorrow, except that she was sweeter and gentler. It is no wonder that everyone who came near her loved her; for there was a mysterious loveliness about her like the mystery of light, not of darkness. She

28

was, I have always thought, as much of an angel as it is possible for a woman to be on this earth. And yet, angelic as she was, there were times when it seemed to me that she both hated and feared her husband. Though he never entered her room while I was there, and I never heard his name on her lips until an hour before the end, still I could tell by the look of terror in her face whenever his step passed down the hall that her very soul shivered at his approach.

During the whole month I did not see the child again, though one night, when I came suddenly into Mrs. Maradick's room, I found a little garden, such as children make out of pebbles and bits of box, on the window-sill. I did not mention it to Mrs. Maradick, and a little later, as the maid lowered the shades, I noticed that the garden had vanished. Since then I have often wondered if the child were invisible only to the rest of us, and if her mother still saw her. But there was no way of finding out except by questioning, and Mrs. Maradick was so well and patient that I hadn't the heart to question. Things couldn't have been better with her than they were, and I was beginning to tell myself that she might soon go out for an airing, when the end came so suddenly.

It was a mild January day—the kind of day that brings the foretaste of spring in the middle of winter, and when I came downstairs in the after-

29

noon, I stopped a minute by the window at the end of the hall to look down on the box maze in the garden. There was an old fountain, bearing two laughing boys in marble, in the centre of the gravelled walk, and the water, which had been turned on that morning for Mrs. Maradick's pleasure, sparkled now like silver as the sunlight splashed over it. I had never before felt the air quite so soft and springlike in January; and I thought, as I gazed down on the garden, that it would be a good idea for Mrs. Maradick to go out and bask for an hour or so in the sunshine. It seemed strange to me that she was never allowed to get any fresh air except the air that came through her windows.

When I went into her room, however, I found that she had no wish to go out. She was sitting, wrapped in shawls, by the open window, which looked down on the fountain; and as I entered she glanced up from a little book she was reading. A pot of daffodils stood on the window-sill—she was very fond of flowers and we tried always to keep some growing in her room.

"Do you know what I am reading, Miss Randolph?" she asked in her soft voice; and she read aloud a verse while I went over to the candle-stand to measure out a dose of medicine.

"'If thou hast two loaves of bread, sell one and buy daffodils, for bread nourisheth the body, but

30

daffodils delight the soul.' That is very beautiful, don't you think so?"

I said "Yes," that it was beautiful; and then I asked her if she wouldn't go downstairs and walk about in the garden.

"He wouldn't like it," she answered; and it was the first time she had mentioned her husband to me since the night I came to her. "He doesn't want me to go out."

I tried to laugh her out of the idea; but it was no use, and after a few minutes I gave up and began talking of other things. Even then it did not occur to me that her fear of Doctor Maradick was anything but a fancy. I could see, of course, that she wasn't out of her head; but sane persons, I knew, sometimes have unaccountable prejudices, and I accepted her dislike as a mere whim or aversion. I did not understand then and—I may as well confess this before the end comes—I do not understand any better to-day. I am writing down the things I actually saw, and I repeat that I have never had the slightest twist in the direction of the miraculous.

The afternoon slipped away while we talked— she talked brightly when any subject came up that interested her—and it was the last hour of day— that grave, still hour when the movement of life seems to droop and falter for a few precious min- utes—that brought us the thing I had dreaded

31

silently since my first night in the house. I remember that I had risen to close the window, and
was leaning out for a breath of the mild air, when
there was the sound of steps, consciously softened,
in the hall outside, and Doctor Brandon's usual
knock fell on my ears. Then, before I could
cross the room, the door opened, and the doctor
entered with Miss Peterson. The day nurse, I
knew, was a stupid woman; but she had never appeared to me so stupid, so armoured and encased
in her professional manner, as she did at that
moment.

"I am glad to see that you are taking the air."
As Doctor Brandon came over to the window, I
wondered maliciously what devil of contradictions
had made him a distinguished specialist in nervous
diseases.

"Who was the other doctor you brought this
morning?" asked Mrs. Maradick gravely; and that
was all I ever heard about the visit of the second
alienist.

"Someone who is anxious to cure you." He
dropped into a chair beside her and patted her
hand with his long, pale fingers. "We are so
anxious to cure you that we want to send you away
to the country for a fortnight or so. Miss Peterson has come to help you to get ready, and I've
kept my car waiting for you. There couldn't be
a nicer day for a trip, could there?"

THE SHADOWY THIRD

The moment had come at last. I knew at once what he meant, and so did Mrs. Maradick. A wave of colour flowed and ebbed in her thin cheeks, and I felt her body quiver when I moved from the window and put my arms on her shoulders. I was aware again, as I had been aware that evening in Doctor Maradick's study, of a current of thought that beat from the air around into my brain. Though it cost me my career as a nurse and my reputation for sanity, I knew that I must obey that invisible warning.

"You are going to take me to an asylum," said Mrs. Maradick.

He made some foolish denial or evasion; but before he had finished I turned from Mrs. Maradick and faced him impulsively. In a nurse this was flagrant rebellion, and I realized that the act wrecked my professional future. Yet I did not care—I did not hesitate. Something stronger than I was driving me on.

"Doctor Brandon," I said, "I beg you—I implore you to wait until to-morrow. There are things I must tell you."

A queer look came into his face, and I understood, even in my excitement, that he was mentally deciding in which group he should place me—to which class of morbid manifestations I must belong.

"Very well, very well, we will hear everything," he replied soothingly; but I saw him glance at

33

Miss Peterson, and she went over to the wardrobe for Mrs. Maradick's fur coat and hat.

Suddenly, without warning, Mrs. Maradick threw the shawls away from her, and stood up. "If you send me away," she said, "I shall never come back. I shall never live to come back."

The grey of twilight was just beginning, and while she stood there, in the dusk of the room, her face shone out as pale and flower-like as the daffodils on the window-sill. "I cannot go away!" she cried in a sharper voice. "I cannot go away from my child!"

I saw her face clearly; I heard her voice; and then—the horror of the scene sweeps back over me!—I saw the door open slowly and the little girl run across the room to her mother. I saw the child lift her little arms, and I saw the mother stoop and gather her to her bosom. So closely locked were they in that passionate embrace that their forms seemed to mingle in the gloom that enveloped them.

"After this can you doubt?" I threw out the words almost savagely—and then, when I turned from the mother and child to Doctor Brandon and Miss Peterson, I knew breathlessly—oh, there was a shock in the discovery!—that they were blind to the child. Their blank faces revealed the consternation of ignorance, not of conviction. They had seen nothing except the vacant arms of the mother and the swift, erratic gesture with which she stooped to embrace some invisible presence. Only my vision—and I have asked myself since if the power of sympathy enabled me to penetrate the web of material fact and see the spiritual form of the child—only my vision was not blinded by the clay through which I looked.

"After this can you doubt?" Doctor Brandon had flung my words back to me. Was it his fault, poor man, if life had granted him only the eyes of flesh? Was it his fault if he could see only half of the thing there before him?

But they couldn't see, and since they couldn't see I realized that it was useless to tell them. Within an hour they took Mrs. Maradick to the asylum; and she went quietly, though when the time came for parting from me she showed some faint trace of feeling. I remember that at the last, while we stood on the pavement, she lifted her black veil, which she wore for the child, and said: "Stay with her, Miss Randolph, as long as you can. I shall never come back."

Then she got into the car and was driven off, while I stood looking after her with a sob in my throat. Dreadful as I felt it to be, I didn't, of course, realize the full horror of it, or I couldn't have stood there quietly on the pavement. I didn't realize it, indeed, until several months afterwards when word came that she had died in the

35

asylum. I never knew what her illness was, though I vaguely recall that something was said about "heart failure"—a loose enough term. My own belief is that she died simply of the terror of life.

To my surprise Doctor Maradick asked me to stay on as his office nurse after his wife went to Rosedale; and when the news of her death came there was no suggestion of my leaving. I don't know to this day why he wanted me in the house. Perhaps he thought I should have less opportunity to gossip if I stayed under his roof; perhaps he still wished to test the power of his charm over me. His vanity was incredible in so great a man. I have seen him flush with pleasure when people turned to look at him in the street, and I know that he was not above playing on the sentimental weakness of his patients. But he was magnificent, heaven knows! Few men, I imagine, have been the objects of so many foolish infatuations.

The next summer Doctor Maradick went abroad for two months, and while he was away I took my vacation in Virginia. When we came back the work was heavier than ever—his reputation by this time was tremendous—and my days were so crowded with appointments, and hurried flittings to emergency cases, that I had scarcely a minute left in which to remember poor Mrs. Maradick. Since the afternoon when she went to the asylum

36

the child had not been in the house; and at last I was beginning to persuade myself that the little figure had been an optical illusion—the effect of shifting lights in the gloom of the old rooms— not the apparition I had once believed it to be. It does not take long for a phantom to fade from the memory—especially when one leads the active and methodical life I was forced into that winter. Perhaps—who knows?—(I remember telling myself) the doctors may have been right, after all, and the poor lady may have actually been out of her mind. With this view of the past, my judgment of Doctor Maradick insensibly altered. It ended, I think, in my acquitting him altogether. And then, just as he stood clear and splendid in my verdict of him, the reversal came so precipitately that I grow breathless now whenever I try to live it over again. The violence of the next turn in affairs left me, I often fancy, with a perpetual dizziness of the imagination.

It was in May that we heard of Mrs. Maradick's death, and exactly a year later, on a mild and fragrant afternoon, when the daffodils were blooming in patches around the old fountain in the garden, the housekeeper came into the office, where I lingered over some accounts, to bring me news of the doctor's approaching marriage.

"It is no more than we might have expected," she concluded rationally. "The house must be lonely for him—he is such a sociable man. But I can't help feeling," she brought out slowly after a pause in which I felt a shiver pass over me, "I can't help feeling that it is hard for that other woman to have all the money poor Mrs. Maradick's first husband left her."

"There is a great deal of money, then?" I asked curiously.

"A great deal." She waved her hand, as if words were futile to express the sum. "Millions and millions!"

"They will give up this house, of course?"

"That's done already, my dear. There won't be a brick left of it by this time next year. It's to be pulled down and an apartment-house built on the ground."

Again the shiver passed over me. I couldn't bear to think of Mrs. Maradick's old home falling to pieces.

"You didn't tell me the name of the bride," I said. "Is she someone he met while he was in Europe?"

"Dear me, no! She is the very lady he was engaged to before he married Mrs. Maradick, only she threw him over, so people said, because he wasn't rich enough. Then she married some lord or prince from over the water; but there was a divorce, and now she has turned again to her old lover. He is rich enough now, I guess, even for her!"

38

THE SHADOWY THIRD

It was all perfectly true, I suppose; it sounded as plausible as a story out of a newspaper; and yet while she told me I felt, or dreamed that I felt, a sinister, an impalpable hush in the air. I was nervous, no doubt; I was shaken by the suddenness with which the housekeeper had sprung her news on me; but as I sat there I had quite vividly an impression that the old house was listening—that there was a real, if invisible, presence somewhere in the room or the garden. Yet, when an instant afterwards I glanced through the long window which opened down to the brick terrace, I saw only the faint sunshine over the deserted garden, with its maze of box, its marble fountain, and its patches of daffodils.

The housekeeper had gone—one of the servants, I think, came for her—and I was sitting at my desk when the words of Mrs. Maradick on that last evening floated into my mind. The daffodils brought her back to me; for I thought, as I watched them growing, so still and golden in the sunshine, how she would have enjoyed them. Almost unconsciously I repeated the verse she had read to me:

"If thou hast two loaves of bread, sell one and buy daffodils"—and it was at this very instant, while the words were still on my lips, that I turned my eyes to the box maze, and saw the child skipping rope along the gravelled path to the fountain.

THE SHADOWY THIRD

Quite distinctly, as clear as day, I saw her come, with what children call the dancing step, between the low box borders to the place where the daffodils bloomed by the fountain. From her straight brown hair to her frock of Scotch plaid and her little feet, which twinkled in white socks and black slippers over the turning rope, she was as real to me as the ground on which she trod or the laughing marble boys under the splashing water. Starting up from my chair, I made a single step to the terrace. If I could only reach her—only speak to her—I felt that I might at last solve the mystery. But with the first flutter of my dress on the terrace, the airy little form melted into the quiet dusk of the maze. Not a breath stirred the daffodils, not a shadow passed over the sparkling flow of the water; yet, weak and shaken in every nerve, I sat down on the brick step of the terrace and burst into tears. I must have known that something terrible would happen before they pulled down Mrs. Maradick's home.

The doctor dined out that night. He was with the lady he was going to marry, the housekeeper told me; and it must have been almost midnight when I heard him come in and go upstairs to his room. I was downstairs because I had been unable to sleep, and the book I wanted to finish I had left that afternoon in the office. The book— I can't remember what it was—had seemed to me

40

very exciting when I began it in the morning; but after the visit of the child I found the romantic novel as dull as a treatise on nursing. It was impossible for me to follow the lines, and I was on the point of giving up and going to bed, when Doctor Maradick opened the front door with his latch-key and went up the staircase. "There can't be a bit of truth in it." I thought over and over again as I listened to his even step ascending the stairs. "There can't be a bit of truth in it." And yet, though I assured myself that "there couldn't be a bit of truth in it," I shrank, with a creepy sensation, from going through the house to my room in the third storey. I was tired out after a hard day, and my nerves must have reacted morbidly to the silence and the darkness. For the first time in my life I knew what it was to be afraid of the unknown, of the unseen; and while I bent over my book, in the glare of the electric light, I became conscious presently that I was straining my senses for some sound in the spacious emptiness of the rooms overhead. The noise of a passing motor-car in the street jerked me back from the intense hush of expectancy; and I can recall the wave of relief that swept over me as I turned to my book again and tried to fix my distracted mind on its pages.

I was still sitting there when the telephone on my desk rang, with what seemed to my overwrought

41

nerves a startling abruptness, and the voice of the superintendent told me hurriedly that Doctor Maradick was needed at the hospital. I had become so accustomed to these emergency calls in the night that I felt reassured when I had rung up the doctor in his room and had heard the hearty sound of his response. He had not yet undressed, he said, and would come down immediately while I ordered back his car, which must just have reached the garage.

"I'll be with you in five minutes!" he called as cheerfully as if I had summoned him to his wedding.

I heard him cross the floor of his room; and before he could reach the head of the staircase, I opened the door and went out into the hall in order that I might turn on the light and have his hat and coat waiting. The electric button was at the end of the hall, and as I moved towards it, guided by the glimmer that fell from the landing above, I lifted my eyes to the staircase, which climbed dimly, with its slender mahogany balustrade, as far as the third storey. Then it was, at the very moment when the doctor, humming gaily, began his quick descent of the steps, that I distinctly saw—I will swear to this on my deathbed—a child's skipping-rope lying loosely coiled, as if it had dropped from a careless little hand, in the bend of the staircase. With a spring I had reached the electric button, flooding the hall with light; but as I did so, while my arm was still outstretched behind me, I heard the humming voice change to a cry of surprise or terror, and the figure on the staircase tripped heavily and stumbled with groping hands into emptiness. The scream of warning died in my throat while I watched him pitch forward down the long flight of stairs to the floor at my feet. Even before I bent over him, before I wiped the blood from his brow and felt for his silent heart, I knew that he was dead.

Something—it may have been, as the world believes, a misstep in the dimness, or it may have been, as I am ready to bear witness, an invisible judgment—something had killed him at the very moment when he most wanted to live.

43

WHEN IT HAPPENS [1]

By JAMES HOPPER

(From *Harper's Magazine*)

A S I came across Sam Nolan the other day he pounced upon me eagerly. "Just the man I want to see!" he cried. "I've been looking for you, I've got something for you. Something you can use, something good this time. I've had my appendix cut out!"

"Yes?" I said, a bit guardedly. Out of an unbounded admiration for my craft and a touching wistfulness to help, he is ever coming to me with subjects for my pen. "Oh, I've got a story for you," he'll say. "You know the Grand Central Station? Lots of people swirling around—some arriving, some departing—trains tooting. Why don't you write a story about that?" No, he is not quite that bad. But almost.

"Come to lunch with me," he said heartily. "I have an hour. I'll tell you all about it. All about my appendix and the hospital and everything."

So we sat at a small table in a quiet corner of the club's dining room, and he began to tell me about his appendix and the hospital and everything. And after a while I found myself waking to the fact that he was really giving me something this time. A bit in spite of himself, as it were. Giving me more than he knew. Because, as he talked, weighing every detail in his painstaking desire to be of service to me, I was seeing what he did not see: I was seeing his wife, his terrible wife.

He never sees her, of course (not as she is); but we, his friends, ever do. And we call her "terrible," using the word not in the classical sense, but rather in the colloquial—which holds less meaning—and yet so much more. His terrible wife.

She rides poor Sam; she sits upon his head; she weighs upon him, a mountain of unrelenting purpose. She it is who is re-

[1] Copyright, 1927, by Harper & Brothers.
Copyright, 1927, by James Hopper.
158

Reprinted from *The Best Short Stories of 1927* and *The Yearbook of the American Short Story*, Edward O'Brien, ed. (New York: Dodd, Mead & Co., 1927), pp. 158–68

sponsible for all these rows and rows of ugly houses with which assiduously he warts the plains, while plaintive somewhere within him still dwells the ghost of the dream of the House Beautiful. She it is who holds him to an undeviating pursuit of the dollar, in a welter of affairs, in a deafening boiler-factory of ignoble complications, while he, poor man, now and then still wistfully thinks that, with the children almost grown, the pressure relaxing, he might gradually reduce his business a little, and have leisure once in a while to read a book (he had a wistful respect for books), or once more to play the flute (he played it very well before marriage, and would like to play it again).

Of course, we all know he will never, never play the flute again; that he is in for life.

That is what I was seeing all the while as he conscientiously told me all about the cutting-out of his appendix; and that is what he was not seeing at all.

On the morning preceding the day set by his surgeon for the operation he had slipped over to the hospital all alone, "without a soul knowing of it." His family, his wife, were at the seaside for the summer; he did not wish to worry them. Once in his room in the hospital, however, he had felt very lonely. "Every one seemed so far away," he said. He had almost revolted, walked out. But by this time he was no longer owning himself. He was in a huge machine, things were being done to him as though he did not own himself. At regular intervals he was made to swallow an unexplained pill. Lunch was brought and he was commanded to eat. He was ordered to bed. A barber came and shaved him. A steward scrubbed him with antiseptics. He was caught in a machine, in a funnel, sliding down toward the thing awaiting him in the morning.

He felt far, far from everybody, far, far from the mild sunshine of what had been his life, but he made no move; it did not even occur to him it was possible to get out of the funnel.

Then in the morning they had placed him in a little low chair with casters and had swiftly rolled him along long halls to the white operating room. The feeling of being in the funnel had increased; he was now in the last little narrow part of the funnel. His loneliness had become a desolation; he felt like raising a shout, anything, toward the outside. Instead, he had carefully adopted an attitude of brisk jollity. Inside the operating room every one was sheeted in white, with white turbans and looked like fantastic giants. He was lifted to the table, the mask was placed over his face.

"And then," he said, "I took a back-flip into eternity. That's just what it felt like—a prodigious back-flip down and through eternity."

When he returned from this interesting voyage he was a dryad petrified in a tree. He was all of stone, and the only part of him he could move was the lid of one of his eyes which he could just barely raise. And across this slit of vision something was passing to and fro like the wing of a gull. White, light, flitting, like the wing of a gull.

It became a cap. The cap passed to and fro. It vanished, returned, vanished. Suddenly it reappeared, very large now, quite near, and a voice "sweet as a chime of low bells" (that is the expression he used, Mr. Sam Nolan) sounded a phrase, "Are you in pain?"

Immediately he tried to reassume the pose which had been his last effort. "Is it out?" he asked, in a manner jolly and brisk— and was shocked to hear only a sort of dismal murmuring.

"Yes," said the voice sweet as chimes. "It's all over. But are you in pain?"

A gentle solicitude was about him like a haze; he did not want to show off at all now; he wished to answer with faith and with truth. Was he in pain? Was this pain he was feeling? One fact was evident: he was stretched out like the four points of the compass in the exact center of a clearing, under a broiling sun, pinned there by a stake driven through his body. A long moment of fixed thinking rid him at length of the clearing and the sun. He was not in a clearing, beneath the sun; he was in the hospital, beneath a roof. Back in his bed. But to that bed he was pinned like a butterfly; nailed by a spike that went through him, the mattress, and down into the floor.

"Not so much pain," he answered, "as some sort of very certain discomfort."

He immediately became very proud of that phrase. He had pronounced it just right; with an English accent.

When Sam Nolan had reached this point in the recital of his adventure (men get their adventure as they may) he abruptly stopped and looked at me with his good, honest, slightly bulging eyes. We had begun lunch late, so that by now we were nearly alone in the big darkish room. "Is all this any good to you?" he asked anxiously. "Are you getting anything you can use? Shall I go on?"

And I saw that what he had told me so far was not what he had been eager to tell me. He had thrown it in for good measure, out of a desire that I should miss nothing—perhaps, also, as a delay. What he really had been eager to tell me he had come to now. But he had fallen into the throes of a doubt, of an embarrassment. His honest face was flushed, he smiled in a forced way.

"Why, you are giving me a lot," I cried encouragingly. "Please go on!"

It was hard, I could see that. But finally he had leaped the hurdle. "Well," he said, "I found out something else which might be of use to you. It's—you know, how in the papers, every now and then, you read about a man falling in love—in love with his nurse. Well, that's it. I think I know pretty well how it happens, when it *does* happen—"

I was looking at him steadily, and he made a sudden little gesture of denial, half frightened, half violent. "Not that I did, of course!" he cried stoutly. "I didn't fall in love with my nurse. No! I'm an old married man. *You* know, John, how close Clare and I are. But you understand that I mean—you see it in the paper every once in a while—how some man falls in love with his nurse. Well, while I was in the hospital a little thing occurred which gave me somewhat of an idea as to how that sort of thing might happen!

"It's partly the dope," he went on hurriedly. "The dope, of course, has a lot to do with it. You see, you're pretty well full of morphine after an operation. And it's also the temperature: you nearly always have a temperature. You're sort of out of your head, you're not normal—*that's* how it happens! Oh, I've got a pretty good idea of how it happens, when it does happen!"

"Go on," I said.

He went on. That first day after the operation had been a

hard one. He had suffered discomfort and pain and semi-delirium.

"I kept making a rule in my head, over and over again. A rule for future guidance. Do you know what it was? 'No operation, however successful, is worth the trouble.' I kept saying that to myself over and over again.

"I kept doing something else, too. My watch was on the stand at my side. I'd look at it, then lie back. Then when I thought two hours had gone by, I'd look at the watch again—and only two minutes would have passed. Two *minutes*, not hours!

"Then I'd say to myself, 'I won't stand it. Each minute is just like an hour, and there are so many minutes! I'm going to throw myself out of the window!'

"But then I wouldn't throw myself out of the window, but just lie there. And after a while I'd think, 'Now, surely two hours have gone by,' and I'd look, and again it would be two minutes. 'I won't stand it,' I'd say. 'I'm going to throw myself out of the window.' But I wouldn't."

It was during the interminable stretching of this burning, tossing, enfevered misery that her coolness slowly established itself about him and filtered into him. Her coolness. The coolness of her voice "sweet as chimes." Of her white starched garments, of her light hands. Of her efficiency.

Her efficiency! He waxed quite lyric over that. I wish I could remember all he said; but I was so stupefied by this spectacle of my business man suddenly run poetically amuck that I sat there staring, marvelling at the miracle without registering. One of his phrases I still recall—"The beauty of efficiency."

It seems that she had that to an extraordinary degree. It had never occurred to him before that simple efficiency had beauty; now he knew it. He assured me that it did. A beauty cool, pure and white, which aroused in the beholder a tenderness!

Throughout the length of that long, hot, miserable day this had sifted to him, cooling his fever, smoothing his tortured nerves, but it was when evening came, he said, that something peculiarly charming had occurred.

"A little thing," he said, "something, I understand, quite customary to nursing routine—rather to be expected—but which somehow took on with me that night the most unreasonable emphasis. The most unreasonable!"

It had been announced by a series of small preparations, but even at that he had not believed it possible. A cot had been brought in and set up. Later blankets, sheets, a pillow.

Then, suddenly, she had vanished.

"And when she returned," he said, "she had been transformed, she was another being. You see, all day she had gone about in her uniform, white, starched, gleaming, like a light armor. But now she had on soft garments. And on her head, instead of the stiff white cap, was one all soft and smoky-blue, with just one little rose. I can't tell you how enchanting the change seemed to me, all doped up as I was. It was as if while she had been gone she had stepped into fairyland."

Even then, he had not really believed possible what was about to take place. She went about the room in a last ordering of things already well ordered, then bent over him. "Now, is there anything more I can do for you?" she asked.

He answered there wasn't, that he was all right.

"You are sure there is nothing you want?" she repeated, with gentle insistence.

"You know," he said to me now, "with all her efficiency, there was something a little childish about her. Childish and innocent. It—well, it drew the heart.

"'If there *is* anything,' she said very earnestly—and she seemed such a little girl—'you won't be afraid to call me, will you? You'll call me?'

"Then I saw that it was true, really true. That the couch, the blankets, the pillows had been brought for her; that she was going to sleep here, in my room.

"Looking back now, I don't see why I should have felt that way about it. It's done regularly in hospitals. I suppose I was light in the head. But I can't tell you what a wonder and a delight filled me now at the thought. This seemed to me the most incredibly charming thing—that little Efficiency should sleep in the same room with me—the *prettiest* thing!

"She slipped about and put out all the lights, all but one; she shaded this low. Then she slid herself out on the couch, and composed herself for sleep. There was a big white pillow at the head; she took it into her arms and drew it to herself, against her breast; she curled up like a little kitten, and in a jiffy was asleep. Sleeping very quietly, without a sound—*just* like a little kitten!"

He halted, he was searching in his head for a better expression than the one he had used. But he came back to it. "It was the *prettiest* thing, John," he said penetratingly.

"I couldn't believe it," he went on. "Every now and then I'd raise myself on my elbow to make sure. 'She really is there,' I'd whisper to myself. But as soon as I'd get tired and fall back out of sight I'd begin to doubt again; I'd have to get up on my elbow again. I'd stay up that way as long as I could, looking at her over there, curled up on the couch *so* cutely, hugging that pillow. Even as I looked I would not quite believe. 'Incredible,' I kept saying to myself. It was *too* wonderful; I couldn't realize such a beautiful thing could be given to me, an old drab like me. I'd keep raising up to make sure. It wasn't a very good exercise for a man who's just lost his appendix, was it?"

I murmured that it very probably was not.

"All the same," he said, with something like a defiant exultation in his tone, "that is how I spent the night! Getting up on my elbow to look, falling back when too tired, getting up on my elbow again. And I remember it as the most delicious night! The moon came up outside after a while and shone in through the window; it touched her, it made her little corner of the room a little cave filled with fairy light. And she was so pretty and so cute in there, little Efficiency at her rest! So sweet! She was so sweet there, in that light, sleeping so quietly, curled up like a little cat, and hugging that pillow to her heart—I'll never see anything like it again—never!

"The moon moved very slowly, the light remained upon her a long time. I kept getting up to look, getting up to look, and each time a new marvelling at my heart. John, she was so sweet, sleeping there in that little luminous cave made by the moon. I couldn't believe it; I couldn't believe something so beautiful could be happening to me. And thus I spent the night, John!

"But is all this of any use to you? Am I giving you anything at all?"

I came in from far away; I sat there, blinking. "Yes," I said after a moment. "You are giving me something."

"It seems—so strange now," he apologized. "Almost—foolish."

"Go on and tell me more," I said.

But he had come to some sort of block. I could see that. He was studying me furtively, appraisingly. "You really want me to go on? You're not bored?"

"No, I'm not bored!" I said.

"What I wanted to tell you about next," he started doubtfully, "is something that occurred three days later. But—well—I don't know—

"You see, I was still a bit out of my head—I want you to remember that. And they were still giving me morphine—don't forget that."

It seemed that a well-intentioned friend, learning by chance that Sam was in the hospital, had written to Mrs. Sam about it. And she had come down post-haste on the first train.

It was the third day after the operation and a sultry afternoon. In the afternoon, he explained to me, he would be feeling worse than any other time. He was told that his wife was downstairs, waiting to come up to see him.

"It was then something terrible happened," he said to me now.

He choked a little, reddened, but looked me straight in the eye. "I found," he said, "that I did not want to see her at all."

"My wife, John! I did not want to see her at all!

"I didn't want to see her, I didn't want to see any one at all! I wanted to remain just as I was up there in my little room. Alone in that small, clean, white, quiet world built about me by Marjorie Downe.

"It wasn't only that, John; but there was a sort of despair about it. I tell you truly: I did not want to see her. Wasn't it queer? And terrible?"

She was told to come up; there was a perfunctory knock at the door; she came in and took her place at his bedside.

"I was altogether desperate, John—it was the *queerest* thing! I was trying to hide it from her, of course. I was trying to talk to her in our regular, accustomed manner. But, do you know, I couldn't! I couldn't remember what had been my usual, my familiar manner; I couldn't remember the *tone*. It would come out all wrong, all the inflections wrong. Just as when you miss the right note. What I said kept sounding as if I were talking to a stranger. I'd listen and I'd know I was talking as if to a stranger, and I wouldn't be able to change it, I wouldn't be able to remember the right tone. Everything I tried would twist around into that wrong way, of speaking to a stranger. It was terrible.

"After a time, John, she began to speak of a project close to her heart—that of our building a new house. The old place, you know, has become insufficient. The children entertain now, and they are a bit ashamed of the old place. Perfectly reasonable, all that; we do need a new house. But, do you know, when she began to speak about it I suddenly went quite wild! I felt as if a hole were being punched in my circle—the enchanted circle which had been drawn about me here, which kept all such things out. Everything began to pour in now—all the mix-ups, the complications—just the idea of moving all that furniture, all those books . . .

"John, suddenly I found myself tearing at my hair. Violently, with both hands. In the most melodramatic manner. Such as you used to see in cheap plays. Tearing away at my hair with both hands. In the most *foolish* manner!"

He came to a stop, looking at me with his flat, honest face twisted with a rueful smile. He seemed to have stopped for good. "What happened then?" I urged.

"Well—she—Mrs. Sam—was surprised, of course. Sat there looking at me in amazement. And a little disgust, dare say—naturally! But she saw I was not up to par, was not quite right. She cut her visit short."

The big dining room in which we were sitting was now empty. Curtains had been drawn; even the waiter who had been hovering about our corner was now gone.

"And that was my wife, John," he said, "my own wife! Isn't it strange what a little illness, a little pain, a few grains of some strange drug can do to one? How utterly, for the time being, they can change one? Alter and twist the real and fundamental nature? My own wife, John! Isn't it queer?

"Anyhow, I've told you all. I'm a bit ashamed to have told

you so much. But I've done that because you are a writer, John. I feel that we poor dubs who go about, busy as anything, creating nothing, owe it to you fellows to tell you anything that may help you. Help you to get things right. And now you have an idea of how it must happen when a man falls in love with his nurse— as you read in the papers often. If ever you have to get that into a story, you'll know pretty well how it may happen—"

He was fumbling along the bench behind him, he had half risen. "Yes," I interrupted, "but *you* didn't, did you? You didn't fall in love with your—with—what is it you called her? With Marjorie Downe?"

"Oh, no, not I!" he said hastily. "Why, I am married, John! Happily married—you know how close we are, Clare and I! No question of anything like that for me. But I did get a pretty good idea as to how it happens when it *does* happen, and that's what I've been trying to get over to you. About the morphine and everything."

We had risen, ready to go, cramped with our long stay; we were facing each other in the large darkish place. "How did it end?" I asked brutally.

He made a vague gesture. "It ended—well—just naturally. You see, in a few days the doctor told me I no longer needed a private nurse; the regular staff service would do. Well, the thing was clear, then. A private nurse costs something; I had no right spending a lot of money that way—when it was so much needed elsewhere—besides the cost of the operation and everything, and my lying idle, my business probably going to pots. I let her go."

He looked at me fixedly. "I gave her a pair of gloves," he said.

His eyes were remaining fixed on me, he did not seem to be able to let go. Then suddenly his face screwed up in a quick spasm, and two tears squeezed out of his eyes. He was appalled; I could see he was appalled at this which was taking place in him. His hands reached out and clutched me. He held on to me like a man choking, who wants his collar loosened, like a man with a heart attack who blindly wants to be held up—and as, helpless, I stood still, looking out over his head, pretending not to see, the movement of his body, transmitted to mine, shook me as if with short hard sobs.

There—it was over—he had mastered himself; he let me go. And catching up our hats we walked out together, I and the man who thought he had some sort of an idea as to how it happens when it does happen.

Zone of Quiet

RING LARDNER

"Well," said the Doctor briskly, "how do you feel?"

"Oh, I guess I'm all right," replied the man in bed. "I'm still kind of drowsy, that's all."

"You were under the anesthetic an hour and a half. It's no wonder you aren't wide awake yet. But you'll be better after a good night's rest, and I've left something with Miss Lyons that'll make you sleep. I'm going along now. Miss Lyons will take good care of you."

"I'm off at seven o'clock," said Miss Lyons. "I'm going to a show with my G. F. But Miss Halsey's all right. She's the night floor nurse. Anything you want, she'll get it for you. What can I give him to eat, Doctor?"

"Nothing at all; not till after I've been here tomorrow. He'll be better off without anything. Just see that he's kept quiet. Don't let him talk, and don't talk to him; that is, if you can help it."

"Help it!" said Miss Lyons. "Say, I can be old lady Sphinx herself when I want to! Sometimes I sit for hours—not alone, neither—and never say a word. Just think and think. And dream.

"I had a G. F. in Baltimore, where I took my training; she used to call me Dummy. Not because I'm dumb like some people—you know—but because I'd sit there and not say nothing. She'd say, 'A penny for your thoughts, Eleanor.' That's my first name—Eleanor."

"Well, I must run along. I'll see you in the morning."

"Good-by, Doctor," said the man in bed, as he went out.

"Good-by, Doctor Cox," said Miss Lyons as the door closed.

"He seems like an awful nice fella," said Miss Lyons. "And a good doctor, too. This is the first time I've been on a case with him. He gives a girl credit for having some sense. Most of these doctors treat us like they thought we were Mormons or something. Like Doctor Holland. I was on a case with him last week. He treated me like I was a Mormon or something. Finally, I told him, I said, 'I'm not as dumb as I look.' She died Friday night."

"Who?" asked the man in bed.

"The woman; the case I was on," said Miss Lyons.

"And what did the doctor say when you told him you weren't as dumb as you look?"

"I don't remember," said Miss Lyons. "He said, 'I hope not,' or something. What *could* he say? Gee! It's quarter to seven. I hadn't no idear it was so late. I must get busy and fix you up for the night.

Reprinted from *The Ring Lardner Reader*, Maxwell Geisner, ed., (New York: Charles Scribner's Sons, 1963), pp. 224–235. First published in *The Love Nest* (1926)

And I'll tell Miss Halsey to take good care of you. We're going to see 'What Price Glory?' I'm going with my G. F. Her B. F. gave her the tickets and he's going to meet us after the show and take us to supper.

"Marian—that's my G. F.—she's crazy wild about him. And he's crazy about her, to hear her tell it. But I said to her this noon—she called me up on the phone—I said to her, 'If he's so crazy about you, why don't he propose? He's got plenty of money and no strings tied to him, and as far as I can see there's no reason why he shouldn't marry you if he wants you as bad as you say he does.' So she said maybe he was going to ask her tonight. I told her, 'Don't be silly! Would he drag me along if he was going to ask you?'

"That about him having plenty of money, though, that's a joke. He told her he had and she believes him. I haven't met him yet, but he looks in his picture like he's lucky if he's getting twenty-five dollars a week. She thinks he must be rich because he's in Wall Street. I told her, I said, 'That being in Wall Street don't mean nothing. What does he do there? is the question. You know they have to have janitors in those buildings just the same like anywhere else.' But she thinks he's God or somebody.

"She keeps asking me if I don't think he's the best looking thing I ever saw. I tell her yes, sure, but between you and I, I don't believe anybody'd ever mistake him for Richard Barthelmess.

"Oh, say! I saw him the other day, coming out of the Algonquin! He's the best looking thing! Even better looking than on the screen. Roy Stewart."

"What about Roy Stewart?" asked the man in bed.

"Oh, he's the fella I was telling you about," said Miss Lyons. "He's my G. F.'s B. F."

"Maybe I'm a D. F. not to know, but would you tell me what a B. F. and G. F. are?"

"Well, you *are* dumb, aren't you!" said Miss Lyons. "A G. F., that's a girl friend, and a B. F. is a boy friend. I thought everybody knew that.

"I'm going out now and find Miss Halsey and tell her to be nice to you. But maybe I better not."

"Why not?" asked the man in bed.

"Oh, nothing. I was just thinking of something funny that happened last time I was on a case in this hospital. It was the day the man had been operated on and he was the best looking somebody you ever saw. So when I went off duty I told Miss Halsey to be nice to him, like I was going to tell her about you. And when I came back in the morning he was dead. Isn't that funny?"

"Very!"

"Well," said Miss Lyons, "did you have a good night? You look a lot better, anyway. How'd you like Miss Halsey? Did you notice her ankles? She's got pretty near the smallest ankles I ever saw. Cute. I remember one day Tyler—that's one of the internes—he said if he could just see our ankles, mine and Miss Halsey's, he wouldn't know which was which. Of course we don't look anything alike other ways. She's pretty close to thirty and—well, nobody'd ever take her for Julia Hoyt. Helen."

"Who's Helen?" asked the man in bed.

"Helen Halsey. Helen; that's her first name. She was engaged to a man in Boston. He was going to Tufts College. He was going to be a doctor. But he died. She still carries his picture with her. I tell her she's silly to mope about a man that's been dead four years. And besides a girl's a fool to marry a doctor. They've got too many alibis.

"When I marry somebody, he's got to be a somebody that has regular office hours like he's in Wall Street or somewhere. Then when he don't come home, he'll have to think up something better than being 'on a case.' I used to use that on my sister when we were living together. When I happened to be out late, I'd tell her I was on a case. She never knew the difference. Poor sis! She married a terrible oil can! But she didn't have the looks to get a real somebody. I'm making this for her. It's a bridge table cover for her birthday. She'll be twenty-nine. Don't that seem old?"

"Maybe to you; not to me," said the man in bed.

"You're about forty, aren't you?" said Miss Lyons.

"Just about."

"And how old would you say I am?"

"Twenty-three."

"I'm twenty-five," said Miss Lyons. "Twenty-five and forty. That's fifteen years' difference. But I know a married couple that the husband is forty-five and she's only twenty-four, and they get along fine."

"I'm married myself," said the man in bed.

"You would be!" said Miss Lyons. "The last four cases I've been on was all married men. But at that, I'd rather have any kind of a man than a woman. I hate women! I mean sick ones. They treat a nurse like a dog, especially a pretty nurse. What's that you're reading?"

" 'Vanity Fair,' " replied the man in bed.

" 'Vanity Fair.' I thought that was a magazine."

"Well, there's a magazine *and* a book. This is the book."

"Is it about a girl?"

"Yes."

"I haven't read it yet. I've been busy making this thing for my sister's birthday. She'll be twenty-nine. It's a bridge table cover. When you get that old, about all there is left is bridge or cross-word puzzles. Are you a puzzle fan? I did them religiously for a while, but I got sick of them. They put in such crazy words. Like one day they had a word with only three letters and it said 'A e-longated fish' and the first letter had to be an *e*. And only three letters. That *couldn't* be right! So I said if they put things wrong like that, what's the use? Life's too short. And we only live once. When you're dead, you stay a long time dead.

"That's what a B. F. of mine used to say. He was a caution! But he was crazy about me. I might of married him only for a G. F. telling him lies about me. And called herself my friend! Charley Pierce."

"Who's Charley Pierce?"

"That was my B. F. that the other girl lied to him about me. I told him, I said, 'Well, if you believe all them stories about me, maybe we better part once and for all. I don't want to be tied up to a somebody that believes all the dirt they hear about me.' So he said he didn't really believe it and if I would take him back he wouldn't quarrel with me no more. But I said I thought it was best for us to part. I got their announcement two years ago, while I was still in training in Baltimore."

"Did he marry the girl that lied to him about you?"

"Yes, the poor fish! And I bet he's satisfied! They're a match for each other! He was all right, though, at that, till he fell for her. He used to be so thoughtful of me, like I was his sister or something.

"I like a man to *respect* me. Most fellas wants to kiss you before they know your name.

"Golly! I'm sleepy this morning! And got a right to be, too. Do you know what time I got home last night, or this morning, rather? Well, it was half past three. What would mama say if she could see her little girl now! But we did have a good time. First we went to the show—'What Price Glory?'—I and my G. F.—and afterwards her B. F. met us and took us in a taxi down to Barney Gallant's. Peewee Byers has got the orchestra there now. Used to be with Whiteman's. Gee! How he can dance! I mean Roy."

"Your G. F.'s B. F.?"

"Yes, but I don't believe he's as crazy about her as she thinks he is. Anyway—but this is a secret—he took down the phone number of the hospital while Marian was out powdering her nose, and he said he'd give me a ring about noon. Gee! I'm sleepy! Roy Stewart!"

"Well," said Miss Lyons, "how's my patient? I'm twenty minutes late, but honest, it's a wonder I got up at all! Two nights in succession is too much for this child!"

"Barney Gallant's again?" asked the man in bed.

"No, but it was dancing, and pretty near as late. It'll be different tonight. I'm going to bed just the minute I get home. But I did have a dandy time. And I'm just crazy about a certain somebody."

"Roy Stewart?"

"How'd you guess it? But honest, he's wonderful! And so different than most of the fellas I've met. He says the craziest things, just keeps you in hysterics. We were talking about books and reading, and he asked me if I liked poetry—only he called it 'poultry'—and I said I was wild about it and Edgar M. Guest was just about my favorite, and then I asked him if he liked Kipling and what do you think he said? He said he didn't know; he'd never kipled.

"He's a scream! We just sat there in the house till half past eleven and didn't do nothing but just talk and the time went like we was at a show. He's better than a show. But finally I noticed how late it was and I asked him didn't he think he better be going and he said he'd go if I'd go with him, so I asked him where could we go at that hour of night, and he said he knew a road-house just a little ways away, and I didn't want to go, but he said we wouldn't stay for only just one dance, so I went with him. To the Jericho Inn.

"I don't know what the woman thought of me where I stay, going out that time of night. But he *is* such a wonderful dancer and such a perfect gentleman! Of course we had more than one dance and it was after two o'clock before I knew it. We had some gin, too, but he just kissed me once and that was when we said good night."

"What about your G. F., Marian? Does she know?"

"About Roy and I? No. I always say that what a person don't know don't hurt them. Besides, there's nothing *for* her to know—yet. But listen: If there was a chance in the world for her, if I thought he cared anything about her, I'd be the last one in the world to accept his intentions. I hope I'm not that kind! But as far as anything serious between them is concerned, well, it's cold. I happen to *know* that! She's not the girl for him.

"In the first place, while she's pretty in a way, her complexion's bad and her hair's scraggy and her figure, well, it's like some woman in the funny pictures. And she's not peppy enough for Roy. She'd rather stay home than do anything. Stay home! It'll be time enough for that when you can't get anybody to take you out.

"She'd never make a wife for him. He'll be a rich man in another year; that is, if things go right for him in Wall Street like he expects. And a man's as rich as he'll be wants a wife that can live up to it and entertain and step out once in a while. He don't want a wife that's a drag on him. And he's too good-looking for Marian. A fella as good-looking as him needs a pretty wife or the first thing you know some girl that is pretty will steal him off of you. But it's silly to talk about them marrying each other. He'd have to ask her first, and he's not going to. I know! So I don't feel at all like I'm trespassing.

"Anyway, you know the old saying, everything goes in love. And I—— But I'm keeping you from reading your book. Oh, yes; I almost forgot a T. L. that Miss Halsey said about you. Do you know what a T. L. is?"

"Yes."

"Well, then, you give me one and I'll give you this one."

"But I haven't talked to anybody but the Doctor. I can give you one from myself. He asked me how I liked you and I said all right."

"Well, that's better than nothing. Here's what Miss Halsey said: She said if you were shaved and fixed up, you wouldn't be bad. And now I'm going out and see if there's any mail for me. Most of my mail goes to where I live, but some of it comes here sometimes. What I'm looking for is a letter from the state board telling me if I passed my state examination. They ask you the craziest questions. Like 'Is ice a disinfectant?' Who cares! Nobody's going to waste ice to kill germs when there's so much of it needed in high-balls. Do you like high-balls? Roy says it spoils whisky to mix it with water. He takes it straight. He's a terror! But maybe you want to read."

"Good morning," said Miss Lyons. "Did you sleep good?"

"Not so good," said the man in bed. "I——"

"I bet you got more sleep than I did," said Miss Lyons. "He's the most persistent somebody I ever knew! I asked him last night, I said, 'Don't you never get tired of dancing?' So he said, well, he did get tired of dancing with some people, but there was others who he never got tired of dancing with them. So I said, 'Yes, Mr. Jollier, but I wasn't born yesterday and I know apple sauce when I hear it and I bet you've told that to fifty girls.' I guess he really did mean it, though.

"Of course most anybody'd rather dance with slender girls than stout girls. I remember a B. F. I had one time in Washington. He said dancing with me was just like dancing with nothing. That sounds like he was insulting me, but it was really a compliment. He meant it wasn't any effort to dance with me like with some girls. You take Marian, for instance, and while I'm crazy about her, still that don't make her a good dancer and dancing with her must be a good deal like moving the piano or something.

"I'd die if I was fat! People are always making jokes about fat people. And there's the old saying, 'Nobody loves a fat man.' And it's even worse with a girl. Besides people making jokes about them and don't want to dance with them and so forth, besides that they're always trying to reduce and can't eat what they want to. I bet, though, if I was fat, I'd eat everything in sight. Though I guess not, either. Because I hardly eat anything as it is. But they do make jokes about them.

"I'll never forget one day last winter, I was on a case in Great Neck and the man's wife was the fattest thing! So they had a radio in the house and one day she saw in the paper where Bugs Baer was going to talk on the radio and it would probably be awfully funny because he writes so crazy. Do you ever read his articles? But this woman, she was awfully sensitive about being fat and I nearly died sitting there with her listening to Bugs Baer, because his whole talk was all about some fat woman and he said the craziest things, but I couldn't laugh on account of she being there in the room with me. One thing he said was that the woman, this woman he was talking about, he said she was so fat that she wore a wrist watch on her thumb. Henry J. Belden."

"Who is Henry J. Belden? Is that the name of Bugs Baer's fat lady?"

"No, you crazy!" said Miss Lyons. "Mr. Belden was the case I was on in Great Neck. He died."

"It seems to me a good many of your cases die."

"Isn't it a scream!" said Miss Lyons. "But it's true; that is, it's been true lately. The last five cases I've been on has all died. Of course it's just luck, but the girls have been kidding me about it and calling me a jinx, and when Miss Halsey saw me here the evening of the day you was operated, she said, 'God help him!' That's the night floor nurse's name. But you're going to be mean and live through it and spoil my record, aren't you? I'm just kidding. Of course I want you to get all right.

"But it *is* queer, the way things have happened, and it's made me feel kind of creepy. And besides, I'm not like some of the girls and don't care. I get awfully fond of some of my cases and I hate to see them die, especially if they're men and not very sick and treat you half-way decent and don't yell for you the minute you go out of the room. There's only one case I was ever on where I didn't mind her dying and that was a woman. She had nephritis. Mrs. Judson.

"Do you want some gum? I chew it just when I'm nervous. And I always get nervous when I don't have enough sleep. You can bet I'll stay home tonight, B. F. or no B. F. But anyway he's got an engagement tonight, some directors' meeting or something. He's the busiest somebody in the world. And I told him last night, I said, 'I should think you'd need sleep, too, even more than I do because you have to have all your wits about you in your business or those big bankers would take advantage and rob you. You can't afford to be sleepy,' I told him.

"So he said, 'No, but of course it's all right for you, because if you go to sleep on your job, there's no danger of you doing any damage except maybe give one of your patients a bichloride of mercury tablet instead of an alcohol rub.' He's terrible! But you can't help from laughing.

"There was four of us in the party last night. He brought along his B. F. and another girl. She was just blah, but the B. F. wasn't so bad, only he insisted on me helping him drink a half a bottle of Scotch, and on top of gin, too. I guess I was the life of the party; that is, at first. Afterwards I got sick and it wasn't so good.

"But at first I was certainly going strong. And I guess I made quite a hit with Roy's B. F. He knows Marian, too, but he won't say anything, and if he does, I don't care. If she don't want to lose her beaus, she ought to know better than to introduce them to all the pretty girls in the world. I don't mean that I'm any Norma Talmadge, but at least—well—but I sure was sick when I *was* sick!

"I must give Marian a ring this noon. I haven't talked to her since the night she introduced me to him. I've been kind of scared. But I've got to find out what she knows. Or if she's sore at me. Though I don't see how she can be, do you? But maybe you want to read."

"I called Marian up, but I didn't get her. She's out of town but she'll be back tonight. She's been out on a case. Hudson, New York, That's where she went. The message was waiting for her when she got home the other night, the night she introduced me to Roy."

"Good morning," said Miss Lyons.
"Good morning," said the man in bed. "Did you sleep enough?"
"Yes," said Miss Lyons. "I mean no, not enough."
"Your eyes look bad. They almost look as if you'd been crying."
"Who? Me? It'd take more than—I mean, I'm not a baby! But go on and read your book."

"Well, good morning," said Miss Lyons. "And how's my patient? And this is the last morning I can call you that, isn't it? I think you're mean to get well so quick and leave me out of a job. I'm just kidding. I'm glad you're all right again, and I can use a little rest myself."

"Another big night?" asked the man in bed.

"Pretty big," said Miss Lyons. "And another one coming. But tomorrow I won't ever get up. Honest, I danced so much last night that I thought my feet would drop off. But he certainly is a dancing fool! And the nicest somebody to talk to that I've met since I came to this town. Not a smart Alex and not always trying to be funny like some people, but just nice. He understands. He seems to know just what you're thinking. George Morse."

"George Morse!" exclaimed the man in bed.

"Why yes," said Miss Lyons. "Do you know him?"

"No. But I thought you were talking about this Stewart, this Roy."

"Oh, him!" said Miss Lyons. "I should say not! He's private property; other people's property, not mine. He's engaged to my G. F. Marian. It happened day before yesterday, after she got home from Hudson. She was on a case up there. She told me about it night before last. I told her congratulations. Because I wouldn't hurt her feelings for the world! But heavens! what a mess she's going to be in, married to that dumb-bell. But of course some people can't be choosey. And I doubt if they ever get married unless some friend loans him the price of a license.

"He's got her believing he's in Wall Street, but I bet if he ever goes there at all, it's to sweep it. He's one of these kind of fellas that's got a great line for a little while, but you don't want to live with a clown. And I'd hate to marry a man that all he thinks about is to step out every night and dance and drink.

"I had a notion to tell her what I really thought. But that'd only of made her sore, or she'd of thought I was jealous or something. As if I couldn't of had him myself! Though even if he wasn't so awful, if I'd liked him instead of loathed him, I wouldn't of taken him from her on account of she being my G. F. And especially while she was out of town.

"He's the kind of a fella that'd marry a nurse in the hopes that some day he'd be an invalid. You know, that kind.

"But say—did you ever hear of J. P. Morgan and Company? That's where my B. F. works, and he don't claim to own it neither. George Morse.

"Haven't you finished that book yet?"

Nurse's Choice

By Frederick Hazlitt Brennan

EVERYBODY on J division (surgical) knew that Miss Armistead was going to choose between Joe Trask and Mort Baker. Next to a newspaper office, a hospital is the most gossipy place on earth; and next to the maternity division, surgery has the worst gossips in a hospital. However, a romantic triangle like this one would have been gossiped about anywhere.

The nurses were absorbed in it, because Miss Armistead was a nurse, and popular although too pretty, and because having to choose between two personable doctors is what nurses dream about. Most of the patients were interested because Dr. Joe Trask was chief resident and paid his duty calls charmingly. It was great stuff for the internes, too, because Dr. Mort Baker was a bright young star in surgery and they wondered what chance a nice guy but a mere chief resident would have when the gal actually got around to making up her mind.

Among the orderlies and maids opinion was sharply and pretty evenly divided—the Trask faction holding that their man would make a name for himself, given a bit of time; while the Baker faction, composed of older heads, argued that you couldn't discount a suite of offices full of social register patients or professional visitors watching Dr. Baker operate.

Through all the discussion, Miss Armistead herself moved serenely. A chief surgical nurse has very little time to be hearing or overhearing gossip, even about her own romance. Not even the sharp eyes of Miss Fordyce, her roommate, could detect any favoritism in Miss Armistead's attitude toward Dr. Trask and Dr. Baker. Miss Armistead divided her spare time with almost scientific accuracy between the two suitors. If she went to a picture show on Friday afternoon with the chief resident, it was a safe bet Dr. Baker would be calling for her in his big roadster Sunday evening. On one occasion, Miss Fordyce reported to the nurses' study group around the chart table on J division, there had been a mix-up, with each man insisting it was his turn. Whereupon, Miss Armistead

Reprinted from *Collier's* 100 (11 December 1937), p. 17

had coolly suggested that they both accompany her to the Medical Society lecture.

"She won't try that again, though," said Miss Fordyce, "because both shut up like clams, and Joe sulked and behaved worse than Baker."

"Joe shouldn't have done that," said Miss Douthit, who was only a probationer but knew life. "The other guy is a better actor. Joe better look out."

THE first direct statement to come from any of the principals was reported by Interne Pruess at midnight lunch in the doctors' dining room, and it sent Joe Trask's stock plummeting to an alarming low.

"If you got any bets on Joe," he said, "you better hedge 'em. He's had a row with Margaret about being rude to Baker, and he's talking about bowing out and going off to India for the Foundation."

Seeking comfort, the Trask faction was given another sockdolager by Miss Morath (a patient—fractured pelvis), who had become Dr. Baker's chief champion. She reported that Dr. Jennings, her physician, had heard that Dr. Baker was planning to give up his apartment at the University Club and was looking around for a house in the West End.

The only ray of hope was Miss Fordyce's stout insistence that although Miss Armistead had fought with Joe it was not a final quarrel and could be made up.

Division J, already a-buzz from the tension of the race, was thrown into a turmoil one Saturday night by word that Miss Armistead, their cool and efficient heroine, had cracked.

Probationer Douthit overheard Miss Fordyce telling Mrs. Johnson, chief division nurse, that Margaret Armistead was in her room with a sick headache and, Probationer Douthit insisted, hysterics.

"Joe went and demanded a showdown—that she would not go out with Baker any more, and that rubbed Margaret the wrong way, Miss Fordyce says, and Margaret said Joe was just a boor, and Miss Fordyce says Margaret is on the verge of taking Baker and getting engaged to him!"

Among the patients to whom this dismaying news was transmitted, only one—young Mrs. McGee—remained stanch and unflurried.

"She'll take the one that she knows really loves her," said young Mrs. McGee, "and a girl doesn't get hysterics if she's absolutely sure."

Then, with paralyzing abruptness, the crisis came. On Sunday afternoon, Miss Armistead reported sick. She refused to see Dr. Joe Trask. Miss Fordyce, after several hours, made a diagnosis of acute appendicitis. She forced the admission from Miss Armistead that she had suffered several mild attacks but was too busy to bother.

Miss Fordyce summoned Dr. Trask at 7:21 P. M. by Probationer Evenham's watch. Dr. Trask left Miss Armistead's room at 7:33 P.M. and ordered the operating room for eight. Dr. Trask and Miss Fordyce were overheard in the following conversation:

"Telephone Dr. Baker, please."

"She wants you to operate, Joe."

"I may have to start it, but you get Baker over here as fast as he can come."

"But, Joe, she has perfect confidence—"

"That's an order, Sally."

DIVISION J watched with mounting excitement the events that followed. Dr. Baker was at the Country Club and said it would take him forty-five minutes. Dr. Trask waited until 8:15 P. M., by Mrs. Johnson's watch, and then tried to reach Dr. Penfield, the chief of staff. Dr. Penfield could not be located immediately.

"Go ahead, Joe," Miss Fordyce was heard to demand, "you'll have a peritonitis if you wait—"

"I suppose I'll have to," Dr. Trask said.

Probationer Timmons, one of the scrubbed nurses, sent word that Dr. Trask looked scared to death as he prepared for the operation.

Miss Armistead entered the operating room at 8:27 P. M. by Mrs. Johnson's watch. Dr. Mort Baker arrived at the hospital at 8:39 P.M. and went at once to the operating room.

The dreadful rumor of what happened in the operating room began to spread swiftly.

"Joe lost his nerve and went all to pieces," said Miss Fordyce tearfully. "Baker came in as cool as a cucumber and took over. We tried to get Joe to leave, but he just stood there shaking. Baker called him yellow and scolded him—it was awful. As soon as the sutures were in, Joe keeled over in a dead faint."

After that, the Trask faction mourned a lost cause. The last chance seemed to be that perhaps Margaret Armistead would not be told what had occurred. But that hope dwindled when it was reported that Joe Trask insisted on seeing Miss Armistead as soon as she was conscious.

The closing scene satisfied even J division's taste for the dramatic.

Dr. Mort Baker, smiling and casual, went into Miss Armistead's room. As reported by Probationer Evenham, concealed behind a screen, the final climax was simply excruciating:

"Baker came in and said: 'Well, Margaret, I'd been looking for years for Caliotti type adhesions and imagine my surprise to meet them in your tummy!' And he laughed and kidded Margaret and talked to her about the case like it belonged to somebody else. I could tell Margaret was not taking it so big.

"Then in rushes poor Joe and flops in a chair beside Margaret's bed and says: 'Oh, darling, I failed you. I went all to pieces like a big baby and Baker here had to finish. He saved your life. He acted like a man and I behaved like a big yellow slob. Forget that you ever even liked me!'

"But Margaret just reached over and grabbed Joe's hair with both hands and pulled him down and kissed him and said: 'I know, Joe; I know. I would have acted the same way if you had been on that table. It's just love, Joe! It makes cowards of us all, sometimes!' "

Division J is sending flowers to Dr. Mort Baker on the day of Joe and Margaret's wedding, a touch suggested by young Mrs. McGee.

Old Ironpuss

ARTHUR GORDON

Corky Nixon is doing fine now as editorial writer on a Midwestern paper. He walks nicely with only a cane, and a pretty girl is said to be in love with him, and happiness is hanging there in front of him like a ripe peach. Soon he will reach out and pick it, and all will be well with Corky Nixon.

But this happened months ago, when things were not too good with Corky or any of the other inmates of Ward 7.

If a poll had been conducted among the patients of that particular military hospital—a poll to determine the relative popularity of the nurses—any one of several gay young things might have won it. But for last place there would have been no contest whatever. It would have gone to Old Ironpuss, hands down.

Her real name was Johansen, but people seldom used it. Her nickname, bestowed long ago by some forgotten genius, fitted her to perfection. She was a tall, gray-haired, rawboned woman with a face that looked as if it had been hacked in a hurry out of a block of oak. She had a pair of cold green eyes that showed no warmth, no sympathy, no concern for the welfare—or lack

Reprinted by permission of the author from *A Treasury of Nurse Stories By World Famous Authors*, Sonia Barry, ed. (New York: Frederick Fell Inc., 1962), pp. 205–215. First published in *Saturday Evening Post* 223 (12 May 1951). Copyright 1951 by Arthur Gordon. Renewed.

of it—of fellow human beings. Her voice matched her face: harsh, rasping, sardonic. When she walked through the wards, her spine might have been a ramrod, and if she heard the subdued hisses that sometimes followed her, she gave no sign.

She was efficient; no one denied that. In thirty years she had never been known to make a mistake. And she was a merciless disciplinarian; younger nurses under her jurisdiction were terrified of her. Casualties back from Korea who thought their recent heroism entitled them to exemption from hospital regulations sometimes got a rude shock. If Old Ironpuss happened to be on duty, they were likely to find their normal privileges drastically reduced. In vain they protested to Colonel Gleason, the white-haired senior medical officer. The colonel was a fine surgeon, and a soft-spoken man. But he always upheld Old Ironpuss.

"Hell," said Corky Nixon disgustedly, "I think he's scared of her himself."

He was sitting in his wheelchair in Ward 7 hanging ornaments on a Christmas tree that had been set up between the rows of beds. Ward 7 was not the most cheerful place in the hospital; its patients were mostly frostbite cases—amputees, that is—and a couple of fliers who had been badly burned. But the Red Cross had brought in the Christmas tree, and Corky was decorating it. For one thing, he still had all ten fingers. For another, there was supposed to be a competition among the various wards with a prize for the best-looking tree, and Corky was not going to let theirs just stand there naked and ashamed.

He was a good boy, this Corky Nixon, with more resiliency of heart and mind than most. Frostbite was not his trouble; a land mine somewhere north of Seoul had done a neater job, taking off both legs just below the knee. For a while he had been in the black throes of despair that always come once the physical pain has died down. But he had fought his way back, partially at least, and if the ward had a leader, he was it. He had a portable typewriter set up on a table by his bed. He drummed a lot of his rage and bitterness out through the typewriter keys . . . and threw away most of what he wrote.

While he worked on the tree, the others watched him somberly. Most of the beds in the ward were empty, it was Christmas Eve, and Colonel Gleason had been lenient about letting some of the boys go home. Carefully, tenderly, their friends and relatives had come and wheeled them away. Counting Corky, there were only six left. Seven, if you included Hancock, the new arrival, in the little room off the ward reserved for patients on the critical list. Hancock had just come in that day.

Corky could have been a Christmas guest in a dozen private homes, but he had refused all invitations. He wanted to stay with the boys who couldn't leave the ward. Cramer, one of the fliers, couldn't leave because he was still a mass of bandages, unable to move hand or foot. Friedheim was there because he had shown a tendency to hemorrhage. Armstrong, the other flier, was still in the process of having his face rebuilt; his head was enveloped in gauze, except for three slits, two for his eyes, one for his mouth. Chudnowski was there because he was incredibly clumsy on his crutches. He had already had two bad falls; Colonel Gleason would not let him leave the ward. Finally there was Danforth, the redheaded Vermonter who had stopped a bullet on night patrol and played dead for twenty-four hours until his buddies went out and found him in the snow. Before he passed out, he had had the good sense to shove his hands inside his parka. They were still trying to save one of his feet.

Of all the patients in the ward, Danforth was the most bitter and the sharpest-tongued. Armstrong had a sense of humor and liked to tease Chudnowski, who had none. There were moments when Friedheim could joke about his tragedy in a grisly sort of way ("Look, ma, no hands!"); and Cramer, who was in constant pain, did not complain about it much.

But Danforth was always sounding off in his hard-edged New England fashion, and at this particular moment his target was Old Ironpuss. "I mean it," he was saying. "If Gleason won't do something about her, I'll send my own complaint through channels. I remember when they first brought me in here, feeling like hell, not caring whether I lived or died. What do I see, first thing? Old Ironpuss, standing right beside my bed."

"The face that sank a thousand ships," murmured Corky, hanging another silver globe on the tree.

"And what does she say to me?" Danforth demanded. "I understand you're a difficult patient. We have no time for difficult patients here. I'd advise you to bear that in mind!' Danforth looked around, his face red and furious. "To me! She said that to me, lying there with a gook slug through my chest and a couple of frozen feet."

"You ain't kiddin'," said Chudnowski fervently. Only that afternoon Old Ironpuss had relieved him of a pint of bourbon left by some well-meaning visitor, and the memory lingered.

"I've seen some crazy things in my time," Danforth went on, "but letting an old barracuda like that come into contact with battle casualties is the worst. You take that guy in there, now—" he jerked his head in the direction of the room where Hancock was lying—"maybe he'll live, maybe not. It's touch and go, anyway. Now you'd think they'd get the best damn-looking nurse in Christendom, wouldn't you? Have her sit by him day and night. Hold his hand . . . If he's still got a hand. Stroke his forehead, anyway. Make him feel there's something to live for. But do they do it? Hell, no! They give him Old Ironpuss. It's enough to finish the guy off!"

"Aw, pipe down," muttered Friedheim. He and Danforth did not admire each other. "You talk too damn much."

"Hancock has Miss Baxter part of the time," Armstrong said through his mask. "She's not so bad."

Danforth's sharp face registered contempt. "Baxter. She's so scared of Old Ironpuss she doesn't know what she's doing! You make a little extra noise in here and you'll see. In she'll come, squeaking like a mouse: 'Boys, boys, please!' Baxter, hah!" Danforth gave a final snort of disgust and flung himself back against his pillows.

Corky finished the tree, wheeled himself over to the wall and switched on the colored lights. He sat there staring at his handiwork. It should have been cheerful, but it was not. He knew why, and he knew the others felt it too. The tinsel, the shining globes, the steadfast star on top—all these things reminded them of other Christmases when they had run, strong, laughing, eager, through their carefree worlds. Now there was only Ward 7, and the contrast was almost too painful to bear.

At about eight o'clock Miss Baxter came into the ward, looking flustered and upset. She said something in a whisper to Corky, and he let her wheel his chair through the swinging doors to the nurses' alcove just outside the ward. There he listened to her tale of woe, nodding sympathetically.

"And he won't take his medication," Miss Baxter said, almost wringing her hands, "and he won't eat, and he won't even answer me when I speak to him. I'm going off duty in a minute, and I'll have to report—"

"All right," Corky said. "I'll see what I can do. But he probably won't talk to me, either. I know pretty much how he feels." He spun himself around. "Open the door for me, will you?"

Miss Baxter opened the door to the room where Hancock was lying, and Corky rolled his wheel chair in. Hancock was fully conscious; his eyes were open. But he was staring straight at the ceiling and his mouth was a thin gray line.

Corky said, not hoping for anything, "How's it going, fella?"

Hancock's eyes remained blank, indifferent. He said nothing.

Corky eased his wheel chair a little closer. "Look," he said, "I know how it is. It's tough. You think you don't want to live, that you'd be better off dead. But it's just a phase you go through. You'll come out of it."

Still Hancock said nothing, and Corky knew how it was with him; all the pain and misery and fear and bitterness screwed down so tight that it was almost like feeling nothing. When you got to that point, you wanted no part of anything or anybody; you just wanted to be left alone.

"Look," said Corky again, trying a different tack, "this nurse of yours is a nice kid. Why don't you give her a break? Swallow your pills or whatever the medicine is. She'll get in trouble if you stay frozen up like this. They'll blame her. I've seen it happen. Her boss is an old—"

He stopped abruptly because the door opened and Old Ironpuss came in. She didn't say a word for perhaps half a minute. She stood there, gaunt and grim, ignoring Corky, staring straight at the man in the bed. Finally she spoke, and her voice had never sounded more grating, "Miss Baxter tells me you're being as difficult as possible. I'm not surprised; you look like the self-centered type. You think you're a martyr, don't you? A noble sacrifice on the altar of freedom! Well, kindly remember you're still subject to military discipline, also that we have no use for cry-babies around here. Think it over . . . if you're not too saturated with self-pity to think at all!"

She swung around, her starched skirt rustling. She stalked out.

Corky sat there rigid, hands gripping the arms of his chair. He thought he had known anger, but he had never known anything like the blast of rage—blind murderous hatred—that roared through him now. To speak like that to a man half dead, a man maimed in the service of his country, a man who had given everything except his life so that this nation could remain serene, untouched, free— He clenched his teeth. Gleason would hear about this! Not later, when tempers had cooled, when excuses might be made! Now!

He whirled his chair toward the door and stopped. Hancock had turned his head. The blankness had gone out of his eyes. Something smoldered there, something that looked like a spark of the fury Corky was feeling.

"Tell her," said a hoarse voice from the blankets, "to take her damn pills and do you-know-what with them!"

It was a message Corky would have delivered with pleasure, but Old Ironpuss was not in the nurses' alcove to receive it. She was not visible anywhere. Corky swore and hurtled down the long corridors faster than was safe in a topheavy wheel chair. He knew Colonel Gleason always worked late; he might still be in his office.

He was. The colonel looked weary. He had operated all afternoon; one of his patients had died on the table. Not his fault, but—

He listened now to Corky's tirade; then he got up from his desk and went over to the window. Sleet tapped with frigid fingers against the pane.

"Dammit, Colonel," Corky cried, forgetting propriety in his rage, "it was inhuman! The woman is a monster, or a sadist, or something! I don't see how you can let things like that go on!"

"What was Hancock's reaction?" the colonel asked, not turning around.

"Why, the natural one, of course! He told me to tell her to take her pills and—"

"Do you realize," the colonel said slowly, "that those are the first words Hancock has spoken in five days?" He turned and eased himself down on the window sill. His face was gray with fatigue. "You're an intelligent guy, Nixon. Why don't you use your head? What's the most dangerous state for a patient to be in? I'll tell you; it's apathy. It's that frozen denial of all feeling, of all emotions because they're too painful to be borne. It's the most dangerous attitude of all . . . because it's only one step from death."

He came back to his desk and sat down. "We face it constantly here. You should know; you had a touch of it yourself. We had to get the patient out of it somehow. We've tried kindness; it doesn't work. We've tried sympathy; that doesn't work, you've been maimed, and you're furious. With good reason, God knows."

He put his elbows on the desk. His hands—his fine surgeon's hands—massaged his face wearily. "We have to get through that crust, Nixon. Before it hardens, before it solidifies. So we reach for the emotion that's nearest the surface. I just told you what it was. Anger. If we can strike a spark of that—just one

137

spark—the life process is regenerated. Now do you begin to see?"

Corky Nixon swallowed hard. "You mean . . . Old Ironpuss—"

"In a hospital," the colonel went on, "there are tremendous emotional forces at work. Illness means pain, and pain means anger, and anger means hatred. So we have our lightning rod, that's all. Very few people know it. I shouldn't tell you, really but—well, sometimes I think Old Ironpuss deserves a break." His eyes rested on the blanket that covered Corky's knees. "You've got your troubles, I know. And you've got your share of guts. But I doubt whether you could deliberately make yourself hated for thirty years, deliberately forego the popularity and respect that could be yours." He paused, then added softly, "I know I couldn't."

Sitting there, facing the colonel, Corky felt his great rage shrivel down to a small cinder. He thought of that gaunt, lonely figure passing through the ward, with the sibilant hisses echoing behind her. He thought of a lot of things. He said, at last, "I'm sorry I bothered you, Colonel."

"That's all right," the colonel said. "I'm glad you did. Go on back to the ward. Encourage the boys to hate Old Ironpuss. That's what she's there for." He stood up. "And another thing: this complaint of yours is an act of defiance. That's good. Get the others to defy her occasionally. We need a spirit of defiance around here." He opened the door. He smiled his tired smile. "And a Merry Christmas to you, Corky."

The gleaming corridor was dim and quiet. The rubber-shod wheels of Corky's chair made no sound. Outside Ward 7 Old Ironpuss was sitting at the desk in the nurses' alcove. Her stiff white figure was in shadow, but light from the desk lamp bounced off the blotter onto her formidable face.

She said to Corky in her acid voice, "Have you permission to be out of the ward?"

"I was talking to Colonel Gleason," Corky told her.

He wheeled himself forward, butted his way through the

swinging doors. The ward was very quiet. From the radio, turned low, came the heart-breaking melody of "White Christmas." Armstrong lay flat on his back, staring through his slits at the ceiling. Chudnowski was picking lint out of his blanket. Danforth was playing solitaire, his face tight and expressionless. Friedheim was propped against his pillows, bandaged stumps crossed on his chest. In the center of the polished aisle the lights on the little Christmas tree glowed steadily.

Corky stopped his wheel chair at the foot of Cramer's bed. "Hey, fellers!" he said. "Old Ironpuss is on duty! Let's do something to annoy her!"

A quiver of interest seemed to agitate the lifeless air. Danforth looked up from his cards. Friedheim's eyes lost some of their deadness. Chudnowski stopped picking lint, and Armstrong came up on one elbow. "What, for instance?"

Corky whirled himself over to the radio and snapped it off. "You know how she hates noise? Well, I know some words to a Christmas carol that you won't find in any of the books. You all know the tune, though. Let's see how loud we can sing it!" He spun himself over to the table where his typewriter stood. "I'll write it out—make a carbon for each of you guys . . . Charley, grab your crutches and swipe five bedpans from the shelf down there. And five spoons."

Chudnowski's forehead was furrowed. "Bedpans? Cripes, what for?"

"To bang on, of course. The more noise the better. Old Ironpuss'll have a spasm, but she won't dare do anything. Not on Christmas Eve!" Corky twirled the paper and carbons into his typewriter. "Wait'll you read this. It's called 'Good King Wence the Louse.' The first verse is kind of mild, but by the time you get to the end it's really rough." His fingers flew; the typewriter sputtered like a machine gun.

Once he glanced over his shoulder. Chudnowski was hopping down the aisle from bed to bed, not bothering to use his crutches. Armstrong was sitting up; under the bandages his mouth was stretched in a wide grin.

"Hey, stupid," said Friedheim to Danforth, "tie a spoon on my foot, will ya? If it'll annoy Old Ironpuss, I can kick the bottom out of a bedpan!"

"A spoon's too small," said Danforth. "Hold still; I'll fix you up with this elegant object." He brandished a small enamel container. "But what'll I use for string?"

"Use the sash of your bathrobe," Corky advised him. He ripped the paper out of his machine and wheeled himself rapidly from bed to bed, distributing the carbons. At Cramer's side he paused.

"You gonna sing, Doc?"

"Hell, yes," said the bundle in the bandages. "Get Charley to hold it where I can read it. I'll drown you all out."

"That's the boy!" Corky wheeled himself back into the aisle, took the spoon and bedpan that Chudnowski handed him, and gazed sternly at his choir. Every eye was on him, bright with anticipation. Gone was the thin veil of melancholy, the gray film of self-pity. They were fired with a single unholy ambition: to annoy Old Ironpuss.

"Ready?" said Corky. He raised his spoon like a conductor's baton. "Let's go!"

Outside, in the nurses' alcove, Old Ironpuss raised her head sharply as the horrid clangor arose. She sat rigid for a moment, listening, then she stood up quickly and walked to the swinging doors that led into the ward.

But she did not go in. Through the square glass windows she saw the fantastic sight, and she heard the equally fantastic words, swelling into a full-throated roar of defiance—defiance—defiance of the worst the world could offer in terms of pain, of suffering, of death.

Good King Wence the Louse looked out
  On the Feast of Stephen!
Someone poked him in the snout,
  Made it all uneven!

Louder and louder the wild chorus swelled, Friedheim kicking his bedpan, Chudnowski thumping with his crutch and holding the carbon so that Cramer could see, Danforth shouting in a shrill, joyous voice, Cramer's clear tenor holding the melody true, Armstrong bouncing in his bed and beating his bedpan with such force that the spoon was bent and crumpled.

Brightly shone the stars he saw,
  For the blow was cru-el
Then a damsel came in sight,
  Riding on a m-u-u-el!

On and on, more and more ribald, waves of vitality crashing out of the void where by right there should have been none, flooding Ward 7, flooding the whole universe, the hoarse unconquerable battle cry of the human spirit.

Old Ironpuss stood there in the lonely corridor, and while she hesitated a thought came from somewhere like an arrow and pierced her heart: "God rest you merry, gentlemen; let nothing you dismay."

Standing there, unable to play her part any longer, Old Ironpuss turned her granite face to the wall. And wept.

T. K. BROWN III was born and educated in Philadelphia. He did post-graduate work in New York and Germany, and was court interpreter during the Nuremberg War Crimes Trials. He is now owner-operator of a resort motel in Florida, is married, and has a five-year-old daughter.

A DRINK OF WATER

FROM *Esquire*

Fred MacCann was a ruddy energetic man, thirty-one years old, with a vast appetite for fresh air and the pleasures of the flesh. He loved golf, hikes in the mountains, great meals of steak and potatoes, bawdy humor, poker; he loved the feel of his muscles working, of sweat on his chest, of the wind over his shoulders, of a woman's body beside him in bed. He loved satiety and the sleep that follows satiety.

He loved above all else women, and it was his hobby to possess them. Waitresses, the secretaries of his business associates, show girls, the wives of inattentive husbands, pickups in hotel lobbies—he laid siege to all of them, with a sort of hearty gallantry, at the rate of about one a week. In springtime he was somewhat more enterprising in the pursuit of this commodity than during the other seasons. He kept in his mind a long and gratifying catalogue of the shapes and behaviour of all the women he had known.

Fred MacCann spent his vacations on the sea, in the company of a woman. He arose with the dawn, shook his girl awake, tumbled her out of bed.

"Come on!" he cried. "The sun's up! Come on!"

She raced him to the surf. They swam as far out as they dared and watched the sea and the land brighten, two bobbing heads. Often they embraced in the solitude of the water, looking back at the white lace of the surf on the beach and at their little cottage. They swam back, clambered up the sand, dried each other with rough towels, laughed and shivered. Later they ate eggs and bacon and made plans

Reprinted from *Prize Stories 1958: The O. Henry Awards* (Garden City, NY: Doubleday, 1958), pp. 179–201. First published in *Esquire* (Sept. 1956). Copyright © 1956 by Esquire Associates. Reprinted by permission of *Esquire*

for the day; they would play tennis, go fishing, maybe dig for mussels around the old lighthouse. In the evening the couple next door might drop in for a little bridge. . . . It was a full life, it satisfied all the needs of his soul.

When Fred MacCann was called to the Army he went, as others had gone, not willingly, not unwillingly; aware that such was part of the destiny which confronted his generation and partially anesthetized by the slogans: freedom and justice. Particularly freedom: freedom was something any man would fight for.

Fred MacCann went to war.

Two years and eight months after his induction he was in a village near Palermo, thirty miles behind the front lines. The sounds of battle were not audible to him; indeed, he had never heard them, had never been shot at nor bombed, and had never seen the enemy.

In his whole adult life Fred MacCann had never felt fear. Anxiety he had known, of course, and, during games of chance or maneuvers in the Army, a kind of excitement that was akin to fear, but never the real fear that sets its claws in the bowels of a man. It was not that he was especially brave or especially insensitive; it was simply that he had never had occasion to be afraid.

He was certainly not afraid of anything when, in the quiet little village near Palermo, he went to a pump for a drink of water and, in moving the handle of the pump, exploded the booby trap that blew off all four of his limbs and blinded him. . . .

But then fear came to him. In the dark months of his convalescence in the military hospital in Algiers and later in the United States Fred MacCann traveled all the dreadful and interminable corridors of fear. He knew, in the vast night of his blindness and helplessness, the whole diapason of human terror.

Pain scatters the forces of the mind: a man loses his focus in its labyrinths. Fred MacCann, a bundle of bandages in a hospital in Washington, was so broken on the wheel of pain and terror that for many weeks his only fear was that he would not get that drink of water from the pump.

"Water! Water!"

They poured it down his throat until he choked, but he did not dare let his mind leave the simple and satiable desire of water, knowing that he had been dealt an injury for which there was no remedy whatsoever.

"Water!"

They realized what was going on inside him and sent him a priest. "Son," the priest said, "you don't want water. You want strength to face the future. It's a hard task, son, but all that lies ahead of you is the future, and you must face it."

After a long while Fred MacCann took the first step from the womb of his defensive obsession and confronted the fact that he was blind. The two coals that lay in his head were his dead eyes: the pain would go, but he would never see again.

It was too much for him. He demanded like a child the right to see. "Take these bandages off!" he shouted. "Let me see! Oh, God, take this blindfold off me!"

The big kids had tied him up and had blindfolded him and were throwing rocks at him. They would put his eyes out.

"Let me loose, let me go!"

Yet he knew quite well that he was blind. No one would put his eyes out any more.

He was weak from such protest when he faced his next fear: that one of his limbs might have to be amputated. It was at this moment in his convalescence that a brave sort of hope began to grow in him. He did not know that both his arms and legs had been cut off, that he was a ruined rump of what he had been. As he lay in bed it seemed to him that his arms and legs were bound fast, and this he bore with patience in his new hope: his bones and flesh were being given time to knit and heal. He could wiggle his toes and fingers and flex the muscles of his calves and forearms; they ached, but they felt strong and supple.

One day he asked the doctor, very carefully:

"When are you going to untie me—let me get a little exercise?"

There was a long silence, and then the doctor said:

"What you need now is rest . . . yes, rest . . ." And then, with a sudden and unexpected pathos: "We are doing everything for you that we can."

"Listen, doctor," Fred MacCann said strongly, speaking straight ahead into the darkness, as he had done ever since his blindness, "you don't have to feel sorry for me. I've had a bad break, I know—I've lost my sight, and I may lose a limb or two—but I've had bad breaks before and I can handle this one. It's nothing to get a man down." His hope was strong in him.

When the doctor was silent he asked a question:

"There's one thing I want to know—how much are you going to cut off of me?"

The doctor was still silent. When he spoke it was with difficulty, and all he said was something about rest and doing all they could for him.

Fred MacCann heard the doctor's quick steps as he hurried from the room, and for two days he cursed him for a sentimental fool. Great God, a man like him could face calamity. But on the third day, while he was thinking these thoughts, he was lifted from his bed and borne away. His limbs had not been unbound, and now suddenly they felt incredibly light, sustained by the air with the same certainty with which the bed had sustained them.

And then he knew. They had been cut off, all four of them. What was left of him was a stump, the minimum blind stump of a living person. If any more had been cut away from him he would be dead.

His hope had planted itself deep in him: the bloom of it withered, but its roots bound his soul to the principle of living. And thus his next fear was not that he would persist in staying alive, but that he would die. Half of him had been cut away; half his body was gone, half his blood. The second half must follow.

"Am I going to die?" he cried. "Am I going to die?"

Soothing hands were laid on him: male or female, he did not know. He knew only that he lay in some sort of crib.

"Death, death, where is thy sting?" he hollered, not quite sure of what he was saying.

Only gradually did the real implications of his condition force themselves upon him. As they did a tetter of buds of fear sprouted over all the vine of his desolation and blossomed with a poisonous fragrance, one by one.

A voice addressed him from the foliage of the vine.

"Never is your word now," it chanted madly. "What you will do from now on is *never*. Aha. This is a story to tell the boys, aha. Well, it seems there was this fella, see, and he could *never*

Swim again,
Work again,
Run again,
Play again.

"He had no legs, this fella, see, so he couldn't
>Jump a fence,
>Ride a horse,
>Climb a mountain.
"And he didn't have no arms, see, so he couldn't
>Hold the cards,
>Swing a racket,
>Strip a woman.

"In fact he couldn't do a thing with a woman, this fella, not even *look* at a woman, because it so happens that this guy happened to be —man, this'll slay ya—this guy happened to be *blind*, so he couldn't even look down the dress of a woman—man, this guy was a *mess*, he was just a thrown-away cigar butt of a guy and, man, he sure was no good for anything, never."

The tight little blister buds of fear burst open one by one and the voice sang its refrain from the secrecy of the fat leaves, a black-face monstrous vaudeville.

"Shut up," he moaned, "for the love of heaven, shut up, shut up, leave me alone, let me die."

"This individual, see, he lived in never-never land," the voice said, beginning its chronicle anew.

Fred MacCann became a child again under the impact of such anguish.

"I can't see," he whimpered. "I can't move, I can't defend myself, I can't take care of myself, I can't feed myself."

The knowledge of his impotency overcame him and he waved his four stumps in the air with a terrible agitation.

"I used to ride horses, jump ditches," he cried. "I used to swim against the tide until I broke it."

"Don't get excited," a strong female voice said, and strong hands were laid on his body. "Calm down now."

"I wish I was dead," he muttered.

And this became his next fear: that he would *not* die. He suffered himself to be fed, but he took as little food as possible, turned away from the spoon that was held to his mouth.

"I don't want any more," he said.

It was the same strong female voice that answered him.

"Eat some more," it said. "You need all the strength you can get."

147

A strong hand took his head and raised it; he swallowed against his will a spoonful of gruel.

"I want to die," he muttered. "I want to be dead."

"You mustn't say that," the female voice said. "You must want to live. Here—" Another spoonful of food was forced upon him.

"Who are you?" he asked. "What is your name?"

"My name is Alice," she answered.

It was by chance the name of the last girl with whom he had spent a summer, and with the recollection of her name came the memory of all the girls he had possessed and of the form of living into which his possession of them had fitted. And now a new fear assailed him: that he would be sent back to that form, to be pitied by the men he had beaten at badminton, to be gazed at with horror by the women he had played with.

"Alice," he shouted thickly. "Alice, don't let them send me home!" He moved the stub of his arm as if to clutch her, for he was still conscious of his missing fingers and could feel them crisping in the air as he sought to touch her. She laid quieting hands on his forehead and chest; and it seemed to him that his arm must have penetrated her body.

The idea of home became obsessive with him. It took the doctors several days to assure him that he would never be sent home. He was to be kept, they told him, where he was now, in the military hospital in Washington, in a private room where no one could bother him, ever. In private they congratulated themselves that it had been so easy to make this prospect acceptable to him.

One after another such fears, these and others, coursed through the frame of his mind. If his mind had been more sensitive, he would have gone mad. As it was, for many months he was prey to a sort of perpetual confusion: it seemed to him often that he was caught in a trough of black racing water, a helpless truncated cork of a man, tumbling downward in eternal terror toward a catastrophe that lay always beyond the next turn of the millrace.

Fred MacCann was a child again. He was helpless as a child is helpless. He needed someone to feed him, to bathe him, to help him in his most intimate necessities, such necessities as he had never supposed since his childhood that another person could perform for him.

"You can do it right here, dear, behind this little bush. No one is looking." It was his mother speaking; they were in a park. He made pipi behind the little bush; then he returned to his mother on the bench and she buttoned up the flap of his trousers. He remembered still the apologetic smile she bestowed on the lady who was watching.

"Manly little chap, isn't he?"

"He's my eldest. . . ."

It was like that now. He needed someone to bring him a bedpan, sit him up on it, clean him after he had used it, carry off the feces— he was a little boy again, he needed a mama to button his panties. Despite his burning embarrassment he was thankful for Alice and her ministrations, as a child is thankful.

She was never coy about these duties, but she was never anonymous. It did not occur to him for a long time that she must be dressed in a uniform, starched and white. He knew only her voice and her hands: her voice was warm and her hands were cool.

"Time for your bath," she said. Not "our" bath, not your "little" bath. *Thank the good Lord,* he thought, *she's a kind, honest woman. Thank the good Jesus I haven't fallen into the hands of some antiseptic fool.*

They took the bandages off his stumps and from his eyes. The doctor was habitually and professionally hearty, a detestable person who called him "fella."

"We're practically well, fella," he said. "Yes, sir, we're just about as good as new. In a couple of weeks we'll be giving the best of us a run for his money. Now we'll just get these bandages off—"

Yes, sir! Yes, sir! Yes, sir! The doctor manufactured conversation, prodded the ends of his arms and legs and put a solution in his empty eye sockets: it lay in his head, two cold lifeless pools, germicidal. Fred MacCann thought: *You contemptible puppet.*

"I hate him, too," Alice said later while she arranged the covers about him. He was unspeakably thankful to her.

It happened to him after his bandages were removed that he was overcome by a dreadful shame because of his mutilation. He knew that people who looked at him saw him as a monstrosity; he imagined that they saw him as an overturned cart with its four red wheels, which were the butts of his arms and legs, turned upward. At such times his shame was so intense that he moaned, cringed and struggled to turn over on his belly.

One afternoon Alice came upon him after such a seizure: he had succeeded in flopping over and was crouching in abjection, his stumps tucked underneath him, in great pain but more at ease nevertheless.

"Fred, what are you doing?" she cried in alarm. He heard her quick steps as she hurried toward him and he felt her hand on his shoulder.

"Fred," she said, "you mustn't do that. You'll open your wounds."

That was all she said, but her hand continued to speak to him, softly caressing his back. It was of his own impulse that after a moment he rolled over, full of a peculiar gratitude toward her.

Gradually he found himself according her the allegiance that a child accords its mother: it was this form that his rehabilitation took. She became gradually the sustaining principle of his life, as a mother is to the child who confronts a still strange and complicated world, one careless gesture of which was enough to destroy him save for her beneficent protection. His wounds were healing: the stumps of his arms and legs were now, to his most inner feeling, no longer the beginnings of limbs of the presence of which he was still sensible in his imagination, but simply his extremities as, before his accident, his fingers and toes had been. He had shrunk in his mind to his proper dimensions. And it was Alice who became his organs of communication. She became part of him.

"You are my eyes and hands," he said to her one day while she was sponging him. (He had lost all sense of embarrassment that she was seeing him naked.)

"I'm more than just your hands and eyes," she answered proudly. "I'm a lot more than that, Fred MacCann."

"Yes," he said after a moment, "you are." He counted off on imaginary fingers the things she was to him. Hands, eyes, arms, legs, feet. . . .

"Over you go," she said. She rolled him skillfully onto his belly and began massaging the muscles of his back.

Decision, judgement, will. . . .

"You are my will," he said.

"I am your will," she repeated. Then laughing: "You are my baby."

They had called the football their baby in the great game with Yale, when the score was tied at the half. The coach had said, "I want you boys to carry baby home to papa," and the trainer had dug at his back muscles with the same energy with which Alice was digging at him now. The whole team had been united with the same heady comradeship and determined purpose; and he remembered having wondered then what the other fellows were made of, what their most private thoughts were like.

"What are you like, Alice?" he asked. "What do you look like?"

"Oh, I look like myself."

"But tell me."

"Medium everything," she said. "Medium tall, medium good-looking, medium brown hair, medium old—"

He constructed his own picture of her. She was about forty-two, broad and solid. Her hair had touches of grey in it and the skin of her face was no longer young. Her eyes were very warm and there was something homey and comfortable about her despite her white uniform. He did not tell her of these thoughts, but they nourished him in his dark prison.

The bandages had been off his wounds for several weeks now, and his day had assumed the pattern that he knew would be his regimen for the rest of his life. In the morning Alice awakened him, removed the sheets and blankets from his bed, and dressed him in shorts and undershirt. She washed his face and armpits, shaved him, and brought him a bedpan, performing for him those personal services that he could not perform for himself; then he sat up and she fed him. During these chores they made small talk with one another.

For an hour after breakfast she read to him, mostly from the newspaper, sometimes from a detective story or a mystery. Then she left him, and for several hours he was alone. It was his practice in this time to exercise: as his stumps became less sensitive he learned to rest his weight on them, to "walk" and crawl, and within the narrow confines of his bed he did so. He learned to execute a primitive bending and turning exercise that kept the muscles of his back limber; and as he went through these motions he thought sometimes of the way the great sinews of his back had flexed and strained when he had wrestled or boxed.

Nevertheless he took pride in his exercises. He noticed how his muscles had knit themselves in his new shape, how their strength was bunched at his shoulders and loins for lack of arms and legs to steer, and he devoted himself to the distribution of this strength over the rest of his torso. He learned how to stand on his head and how to execute somersaults, and when Alice came into the room he cried:

"Look, I can stand on my head!" Or, "Look at that shoulder muscle —see how it's spreading into my back?"

"I see," she said.

And one day she said, "Fred, I'm *proud* of you!" Her voice rang, and he was speechless with thankfulness.

Such an event was a high point in his morning.

At noon Alice returned to him again for another feeding. Afterward she took off his shorts and undershirt and gave him an alcohol rub-down, and if the weather was fine she carried him to a wheel chair, wheeled him down the echoing corridors of the hospital, past other patients whose voices lowered as he came in sight, and out into the courtyard, to the edge of the little pool. He sat like a solemn doll in its carriage and thanked God for the sun.

"Oh, that poor blighted bastard—holy smoke, look what's left of *him.*"

"And I thought I was bad off losin' a leg."

"You thought *you* were bad off—I thought I was cooked with both hands off me. Jeez, that poor blasted sonofabitch."

His hearing had become very acute since his loss.

"Alice," he asked, "what are those two men doing over there—the one without any hands and the one with a leg missing?"

"Why, they're just sitting on a bench, smoking." Then with amazement: "Fred, how did you know—what they look like, I mean?"

"Did you hear what they were saying?"

"No, of course not. They're miles too far away. Fred, how—"

"I heard them," he said soberly. "I heard them very clearly." And a moment later, to break the silence: "Funny how I don't want to smoke any more since my blindness."

"Yes—" she said uncertainly.

He felt sorry for her.

"There's somebody across the pool smoking a pipe," he said cheer-fully. "Right? And there are fish in the pool, and moss, or something— I can smell it. And do you know what we're having for supper?"

"No."

"Pork," he said triumphantly. "Pork and carrots. I can smell the cooking like it was right under my nose."

She wheeled him slowly up and down the gravel paths, and he smelled the grass and the geraniums and the pond, and he heard voices, and the bickering of innumerable sparrows; and he let the sunlight burn into his little body. The sun was something he thanked God for again and again.

In the evening they talked together. He discovered very soon that she was not an intelligent person; but he discovered also her extraordinary sensitivity to his moods and feelings, such that he could lay his heart in her sheltering hands without fear of hurt.

She fed him supper and prepared him for the night, and after supper the doctor visited him briefly, probed his stumps and called him "fella." Alice and he despised the doctor; they were in league against him, partners in a deeper fellowship. After the doctor had left she pulled the covers up over him and opened the window; and she had formed the habit of laying her hand for a moment on his forehead before she left.

So Fred MacCann spent his life. He had laid his center of gravity outside himself, had placed it in this woman who did all his moving and acting for him. When she was not with him he lay in silence and thought about her, and was filled with a great bursting affection for her to which, for lack of arms and legs and sight, he could never give adequate expression.

But he tried, one day, to tell her with his voice.

"Alice," he said, "do you know how much you mean to me?"

She was giving him his daily rubdown and her hands at that moment were kneading the muscles of his shoulders. For an instant they stopped their motion; then she continued her work without answering.

"I've never told you," he said, speaking in the slow reflective way that had become natural to him, "but I want to tell you that you are more to me than anyone has ever been in my life."

"More than anyone?" she asked carefully.

"Yes, more than anyone, because you are actually a part of me—you are my senses—my eyes and hands. . . . I told you that once. . . . You are the part of me that does the things I am not able to do myself. That's why I'm not embarrassed to be naked in front of you, like now."

Her hands had moved down to his sides, and again they lay still.

"I am another person, too, you know," she said. "I am Alice." And she added: "I am a woman."

"Of course," he answered. "I know that. You are—"

He was going to say, at last, that she was like a mother to him, a person whom he loved as one loves a mother, when something hap-

pened to prevent him. For she interrupted him, speaking very softly
words he could not understand; and as she spoke her hands, which
had touched him heretofore only impersonally as tools, came suddenly
alive, began caressing his chest, his abdomen, his thighs. Her voice
sank to a whisper, while her hands strayed up and down the short
length of him, and she continued to whisper incoherent phrases whose
cadence, strangely, was that of a lullaby.

Fred MacCann felt his world, in which she had assumed the position of his mother, deserting him. What was she doing? His first incoherent thought was that she was mocking him, and he raised the
stumps of his arms to cover his face, in a piteous and eloquent gesture.

"Alice," he muttered, "what are you doing to me?"

"I told you I was another person." She was panting. "A woman.
I am loving you, loving you with my hands."

He could not understand that anyone could love him in that way,
ever again; but now suddenly, at her words, a lost hope blazed incredibly in his mind, so brilliantly that it seemed to him he could
never live again if it were not fulfilled. Yet he did not dare say a word.

When she touched him it was with hands that spoke to him
tenderly. *You are mine*, they said; *you are my man.*

"Fred MacCann," she murmured, "what have you done to me?"

He laughed in joy at the idea that he was able to *do* anything at
all, and for a moment he was gnawed by a terrible frustration, that he
was not able to leap out of bed and seize this woman in his arms.

His life did not take on a new shape after this day, but his spirit
acquired a new dimension: confidence. He had regained that power
which, of all his powers, he had prized most highly: his power over
women; and with the recovery of this ability Fred MacCann redis-
covered a dynamic in his living. He experienced an ingathering of all
the energies that his accident had dispersed; his center of gravity lay
again within the limits of his own body and he knew he had been
wrong to believe that the rest of his days could be no more than a
gradual vegetable decay.

In his jubilation that this strength had not been taken from him
he came almost to feel that he had not been damaged at all.

"You thought you'd got me, didn't you?" he said aloud, under his
breath, addressing the imaginary savage who had dealt him this mis-
chief. "You thought you'd put MacCann on ice, didn't you, you lousy

rat? Well, you overlooked one little detail, my friend, you sure overlooked an important little detail!"

He laughed boisterously, rolling from side to side and flapping his
four stumps with great vigor. His exhilaration set him to turning
somersaults back and forth in his crib, as fast as he could.

"Oh, man!" he squealed. "Oh, man, oh, man, oh, man, oh, man!
Cut off my legs and call me Shorty! Damn me for a dirty dog!" he
guffawed, standing on his head and tumbling over on purpose. "Oh,
mother!" he howled, seizing his pillow, wrestling with it, worrying it
with his teeth. "Oh, mama, damn me for a dirty dog, it's too much
for me, I can't take it, oh, man, oh, man, oh, man!"

Under the impact of this experience his picture of Alice changed
radically. She appeared in his imagination now not elderly and
motherly but young and vital: she had the flaming red hair of a re-
ceptionist he had once known in Montreal; her eyes flashed with a
sullen passion, and her body was of cool perfection under the con-
cealing lines of her uniform. It was an image he valued so dearly that
he did not attempt to submit it to the test of reality: he did not
question her again about her appearance.

But his behaviour toward her changed. She was his girl. It had always been his contract with women that he, as the man, was pro-
prietor of the relationship: he was the boss. He began to treat her
with the genial condescension of the man practiced in the manipula-
tion of women. He called her "baby" and made remarks designed to
show that this sort of experience was nothing new in his life.

"Baby!" he cried as soon as he heard her step in the room. "Baby,
come over here and give papa a great big kiss."

She put her tray down; came and knelt by his bed; kissed him.

He bit her arm playfully and caught her breast between the stubs of
his arms.

"You're a good kisser," he said.

She withdrew from him quickly.

"I'm not a good kisser. Fred, you mustn't say things like that."

"Yes, you are!" he insisted.

He felt her arm stiffen and knew that he had hurt her; and somehow
this was a satisfaction to him.

Yet his heart was bursting with love for her. And remorse came at
once.

"I'm sorry, honey—I didn't want to make you unhappy—I'm just a clumsy damn fool. I'm so glad for you I don't know what I'm saying—"

She laid careful, tending hands on him and murmured something of which he caught the phrase "all right."

That was her manner now: to comfort him, calm him, lay her cool hands upon him; to caress him with her quiet voice.

They planned their days toward the moments when it would be possible for Alice to hang the little DO NOT DISTURB sign outside his room and lock the door.

"You are resting," she whispered to him. "You are asleep and you mustn't be disturbed. And I'm watching over you, in case you should wake up and want something."

"I want something," he answered. "I want you."

She laughed low in her throat. And the fact that she loved him was an experience more gripping than any he had ever had in the wholeness of his body.

She took care of him in these days like a precious plant. He had very little time to think, and was at peace. Their companionship so nourished him, it seemed to him sometimes that he had gone to war and had been mutilated simply for its sake. He was not sorry it had happened.

"Alice, do you love me?"

"Fred, if you only knew—if you only knew!"

"How many men have you loved?"

"Not many, Fred; two or three. None of them like you."

"What do you mean by that?"

"None of them—well, no one really."

"Really?"

"No—I—I hated them, sort of—even when I loved them. I never really loved any man, never until you."

"But why me, Alice? Look at me—a ruin."

"No," she said vehemently, "no, no! You're not a ruin! You're a lot more a man for being—hurt this way. You're nothing but man—all the rest of you has been cut away."

Her smell was rutty, like musk. He could hear her breathing: she was drawing air deep into her lungs, through her nostrils.

"What do you mean—more a man?"

"Oh, I don't know!" she cried. "I don't know, I don't know! I just know I love you!"

And her hands were on him again, touching him lightly here and there, almost with reverence.

Later he puzzled over what she had said about his manhood. More a man for lacking his limbs and his sight? He asked her about it.

"Alice," he said warily, "tell me: what do my—stumps look like? Are they red?"

"Pink," she answered calmly. "Baby pink. Shiny new skin."

"Are they round?" he asked. "Like wagon wheels?" A distant memory returned to him, a fear he had once had.

"Wagon wheels? Goodness no. They taper. . . . Fred, what's the matter with you? Are you feeling bad?"

"It's nothing—I just wondered."

He still wondered. More a man? The rest of him cut away?

"Fred, are you ill?" she asked again, and there was a strange quality in her voice. "Shall I call the doctor?" Startlingly she was kneeling beside him, cupping his face in her hands. "You're not sick, are you? There's nothing wrong with you?" There was anguish in her voice now, and he was struck again by her peculiar and intuitive perceptiveness, for in that moment he was beginning to feel uneasy; not sick, not physically unwell; but a yeast of perturbation was beginning to grow in him, a little mold of doubt.

"No, of course not," he said crossly. "I just wondered."

He felt the pressure of her strange concernment and drew away from her. "Alice, for God's sake, what's the matter with you?"

Suddenly she was weeping convulsively, reaching out with her hand and kneading the flesh of his belly. "Fred, Fred, don't get sick—don't leave me that way! I've kept such good care of you, I've tended you. . . . You're my man—don't get sick and leave me!"

He understood her to be saying, "Do not die." He had never felt further from death; her inexplicable anxiety struck him with a disquietude such as he had not known since the first weeks of his hospitalization. Shockingly, he felt his arms again spring light and strong from his shoulders: he made a motion as if to take her hand in his.

"Alice, what is the matter with you?"

It was minutes before she was calm again.

Later that evening, after she had put him to bed, he heard her steps in the hallway, coming rapidly toward his room, and he knew at once that something had happened. She came to his bedside without turning on the light and there was a burning quality in her voice when she spoke.

"They've transferred me," she said. "They've put me off in another building, with the mental cases. I just found the notice in my box. Fred, I think they know about us."

"Can't you appeal?" His heart was beating savagely.

"I've already spoken to Dr. Woodrow; he says they need nurses over there and it's my turn—"

"But can't you tell them that I need you? Holy Mary, you're the only one who knows how to handle me—they must see that!"

"But they *know* about us, Fred—I didn't dare—"

"Don't be a fool!"

His agitation was terrible. He felt in this moment not as if he were armless and legless, but as if his limbs were bound, as if he had been without provocation overpowered and was being submitted to gratuitous and stupid cruelty. His rage turned against her.

"Don't be a fool! How can they 'know' about us? They don't know a thing—some idiot is trying to be important, that's all. Now get the hell back to your Dr. Woodrow and tell him not to be a dog. Send him in here, let me tell him! Oh, Lord, you'll mismanage everything and kill both of us!"

He heard a crinkling of her uniform and even before he heard her sobs he knew that she had covered her face with her hands; and the realization came to him that she was as broken and suffering in this matter as he was, and as helpless. It was too much to bear; he thrashed about until he was standing upright on his stumps and stood weaving in the darkness, unable to express his turmoil any further. Not twelve inches of his arms were left, and he was blind.

"Oh, Fred," she moaned, "oh, Fred, Fred, Fred, Fred!"

"Go back to your room," he muttered. "See about it in the morning. No use trying to do anything now."

He spent the night in treacherous tunnels and in a ruined tower, climbing circular stairs in terror; and just before dawn a flash of lightning revealed to him the ragged end of the stairway and the black pit into which his next step would have thrown him. He recognized the scene from Stevenson's *Kidnapped*, which he had not thought of for twenty years.

In the morning it was a male voice that awakened him.

"Hello, Mac," it said. "Alice got herself a new shift. I'll be taking care of you from now on. My name's Sol."

She has failed me, he thought.

"Where's Alice?" His voice sounded stupid.

Sol was very cheerful and professional.

"Mental cases. The boys who see the rockets' red glare, bombs bursting in air. Some mess. Now—upsy daisy."

He was flung without ceremony onto his belly and a thermometer was thrust up his anus.

"What are you doing?" he cried thickly. He forgot his lack of arms and made a gesture to remove the thermometer.

"Temperature, Mac—gotta see about the old temperature."

"Take that thing out of me!"

Fred MacCann spoke with the dreadful urgency of helpless anger; but Sol was cheerful as ever.

"Relax, old man, take it easy. We gotta take the temperature, every morning. So take it easy."

There was a sharp edge to Sol's cheer, which was sadism: Fred Mac-Cann found that out at once. Sol made no effort to handle him kindly: he treated him like a thing, an insensate object. He let rubbing alcohol get into the sockets of his eyes, where it burned fiercely; fed him perfunctorily; slung him like a sack into his wheel chair. Moreover, it soon became apparent that Sol found a lewd pleasure in performing his loathsome duties.

"You don't know how I enjoy this, Mac, old boy, you just couldn't know," Sol said on the third morning, when he was cleaning up after the bedpan.

This was a sort of possession Fred MacCann had never reckoned with. He suffered worse than he had ever suffered in his life. He told Sol to get him Dr. Woodrow.

"Don't know if I can," Sol answered. "He's a hard man to get. What's the trouble, Mac—something wrong?"

"Get me Dr. Woodrow!"

"You're the boss," Sol said. "See what I can do."

He went out; came back in a few minutes.

"No soap. He's busy."

Without a word Fred MacCann struggled upright in his crib, fumbled his way to some sort of grip on the low railing and began to lower himself over the edge. His grip failed: he tumbled, cracked his head nastily on the floor.

"Hey, what're you doing?" Sol had him about the waist.

"Take your foul hands off me!"

The rage in his voice was so vivid that Sol let loose of him. Fred MacCann began moving like a seal on its four flippers toward the door.

"Mac, for Chrissake—" Sol had him by the shoulders and was pulling back on him. He knew how to handle this sort of thing.

And suddenly Fred MacCann was screaming, like a disemboweled horse, shrilly and with no regard for his dignity, in the utter abandon of his desperation.

"Dr. Woodrow!" he screamed. "Woodrow! Doctor! Help!"

Footsteps ran to the room and departed; excited questions were asked and answered; Sol's frightened voice vanished down the corridor. Then, after an empty eternity, the voices fell still and a single strong voice said:

"Get out of here, all of you!"

Shuffling feet departed.

"I am Dr. Woodrow," the voice said.

The limbless blind man on the floor remembered his dignity; lowered his voice and his passion.

"Help me into my bed, please, doctor."

Hands lifted him to the bed. Silence.

"Doctor," Fred MacCann said with a sort of strangulation, "you've got to get Alice back here for me."

The doctor was still silent.

"Doctor," he said desperately, "you've got to get that dirty sadist out of here and let Alice take care of me. Otherwise I'm going to go crazy."

"Now, now—" Dr. Woodrow said.

"I'm not feeding you any stuff," Fred MacCann said strenuously. "I don't know how near I came to going off my nut while I was getting used to this—condition, but I know I came awful close to it. It was Alice pulled me through. Doctor, I need her like I need air and food."

"Sol won't do?" Dr. Woodrow asked.

"Do? Do?" Fred MacCann became so agitated that he pulled himself erect and began to gesticulate with the butts of his arms. "Why that cheap dirty crud is going to kill me! He treats me like a *thing*—he regards me as his plaything. He—I can't tell you what a—a danger he is to me, but I can tell you this: I've got to have Alice back, I've got to!"

Dr. Woodrow was silent; for a long time the only sound in the room was Fred MacCann's heavy breathing. Then the doctor spoke: "You'll have her back. Tomorrow."

Fred MacCann slept that night with the deep sleep of content.

And the next day, in the hospital garden after supper, Sol was saying, "You sure crossed me up mean, Mac. I never would have figured you for such a louse," when Fred MacCann heard her beloved voice.

"They shifted me back here," she said. "Sol, Woodrow wants to see you in the office."

"Alice!" Fred MacCann whispered.

"The office!" Sol was suddenly very small and ugly. "You cheesy squealer, MacCann, you sure pulled a dirty trick on a guy that liked you and was nice to you. I hope your lousy leg stumps gangrene on you up to your belly button. You broken-down double-crossing cripple."

"Alice!" Fred MacCann whispered again, when he was gone.

"It's me, Fred," she said. "I'm back."

"Thanks be to God! Alice, take me back to the room."

"I thought of you every minute," she said. "Fred, there was no way I could forget you—"

"For the grace of God, Alice, take me back to the room!"

She wheeled him from the courtyard at once, and when they were in his room she picked him up with a strong triumphant motion and bore him to the bed.

"Fred, I have a present for you!" Her steps hurried away from him and returned. "Open your mouth."

She propped him up with an arm under his head and held something to his lips. It was a bottle of whiskey, the first whiskey he had tasted since his accident. He took a deep pull at it: it warmed his bowels with an unholy and wonderful fire.

"Alice," he gasped, "you blessed creature! You know everything!"

"Take another drink," she said, "and another, and another! It's a whole fifth, Fred. There's plenty for both of us. We'll put the sign on the door and we'll *celebrate*—we'll get drunk, we'll have a real orgy!"

There was a fermented quality to her voice. He heard her pouring liquor down her throat; he heard the explosive little exhalation that followed her drink.

"Come on!" she said. "Drink! Here, let me wash you off. A real fire bath." She spilled whiskey into her hand and doused him with it; and this unnatural washing became a ferocious and devouring caress.

The bottle was pressed again to his lips; he drank, and she did. Exuberantly he heaved himself to a sitting position and held out his stumps.

"Alice," he cried. "Come close to me! Let me hold you!"

And this was the catastrophe: that she pushed him back, pushed him back with such vigor that he struck his head against the railing of the bed, and said in sort of ecstasy:

"No! No! Let me hold *you!* Let me hold tight that wonderful thing that you are!"

A *thing!* he thought. A crack of thunder split his head open.

"You're mine!" she panted, seizing him in her strong arms and hoisting him into her lap so that he lay there in her grip like the rump of some monstrous child. "You're mine!" she repeated. "My wonderful man thing!"

Fred MacCann felt a sudden and overwhelming fear, so profound that he was powerless to express it. His dreadful helplessness was at him again, much worse than ever before. He lay in silence while she cuddled him. A poisonous weed began to grow in his heart, the same weed that had sprouted in the souls of Adam and Eve after they had eaten of the apple. He was aware of his shame: he had lost his innocence.

"Oh, Fred! Oh, Fred!" she gasped, clutching him to her like a bundle. She reached over for the bottle, put it first to his mouth, still in her strange state of exaltation, did not notice that he did not drink, and put it then to hers.

She took his head between her hands and kissed his dead eyes.

"How I love you," she murmured. "Fred, I'm going to tell you a secret." Her voice was eager and confiding, the voice of a woman sharing part of her private life with the man she loved, because she loved him so.

He knew that she was about to pronounce the sentence of death over him. With a strong, single and not violent motion he removed himself from her embrace and took up a position in the corner of his crib, seated. His face, as he turned it toward her, felt unnaturally large, as large as all the rest of him.

"Fred," she said mysteriously, "would you suppose I didn't like men?" Her voice was drunken. She waited for him to answer; when he did not she leaned very close to him.

"No, you wouldn't suppose that," she whispered. "But I do. I *hate men!* I hate them all: tall men, short men, all possible sorts of men. I hate them all!"

He heard her words with a bright and lucid terror.

"And I'll tell you why," she went on, her voice really quivering with hatred. "Because I see them looking at me on the street like hungry beasts, looking at my body, figuring how they can get me and—and use me. That's what they want to do—grab ahold of me and use me. Fred, you don't know how I hate it when a man grabs ahold of me!"

She drank again.

"That's my secret, Fred," she said. Then, with a drunken earnestness, "And that's why I can't understand why I love you so. You're the only man I've ever loved, and I can't understand why I should love you."

But Fred MacCann, contemplating in his mind the four pink stubs of his limbs with which he could not take hold of her and the two shrunken cavities in his head with which he could not look at her on the street, understood. A grotesque image of himself sat in his place in the corner of the crib: a phallus; around it the trunk of a body, enough to sustain the life of the organ, no more, no head, no limbs; a phallus on its small pedestal of flesh. Not planted anywhere, not sacred in any way, by no means inviolable: any woman could carry it off and use it. A thing. Impossible that it should ever be anything more than a thing.

"Alice," he said thickly, "I think I've had enough. Drank too fast. Could you please go now?"

Her statement of her love for him had aroused her anew. Her hands touched him again with their old invocation. He felt such a loathing that he nearly vomited.

"Alice," he whispered desperately, "I mean it! Don't touch me—I'll be sick. Please go now. Go, go!"

The quality of his voice arrested her.

"Are you really sick, Fred? Do you want a bicarbonate? Something to settle your stomach? Here, you just wait a minute." She became a nurse again, started to bustle about the room.

It was intolerable to him that she should stay in his presence another moment, but he did not have the strength to get rid of her. He submitted to some medicine, to her hand on his forehead, and then, as she was saying good night, to her lips on his and her fingers in his hair.

"There's some more in the bottle, Fred," she whispered. "I'll save it for tomorrow. Tomorrow I'll come again, Fred, tomorrow. Can you wait, sweetheart? Can you wait?"

"Yes," he answered. "I can wait."

After she left he lay in stupefaction, that this should have happened to him so abruptly. Twenty minutes ago he was as happy as he had ever been in his life; now he was at the end of a road.

Gradually the shock receded; the numb, stupid perplexity left him. But what came in its place was a sickly and hideous shame, a shame that made him faint and giddy in his heart; he wanted to die.

Fred MacCann's mind turned, with a ponderous, inevitable and dreamlike motion, to the thought of the pool.

"Yes," he said aloud.

With the same slow, dreamlike movement he raised his body. His experience of the day before had taught him something; this time he got a firm grip on the railing of his bed, holding it between the stump of his right arm and his jaw, and after he had let his body fall out of the bed he arrested its swinging with the stump of his other arm before he let himself drop to the floor. He landed erect on the butts of his legs and waddled clumsily toward the window, lunging forward first with one shoulder and then with the other.

The window was low and open at the bottom, but there was nothing to get a grip on. He struggled for many minutes to raise himself to the sill. Finally he went in search of a chair, found one by his bed, pushed it ahead of him to the window, clambered up on it, and from it to the window sill.

What is below me? he wondered. *Paving? Grass? Perhaps a basement light well? How far is it? Why,* he said to himself, with a wan impulse of humor, *I might break a leg.*

He backed out the window, holding on as long as he could; then he let himself drop. He hit a ledge about halfway to the ground, fell backward with a great crash into a bush, startled but unhurt. As he hit the ground he grunted as a porcupine grunts when it is hit with a club.

Suddenly a great urgency overcame him: he must get this done quickly. He struggled out of the bush and set out as fast as he could toward where the pond was, stumbling and falling. Night smells were all about him: the grass damp with dew, the bloom of many flowers; and night sounds: the incessant creaking of the crickets, the distant hoot of a train; and ahead of him, beckoning, the faint splash of the fountain in the pool. Twice he smelled roses ahead of him and turned aside before he was caught in their thorns; once he gouged himself cruelly on the prong of a rake lying in the grass.

He tripped over a low iron fence and fell with his face in cinders: the path. He waddled beside it, in the grass, slower now because his stumps hurt him and because he was bestridden with the dreadful weight of death. When he felt the cold flagging of the promenade under him the murmur of the fountain was like the roaring of a waterfall in his ears and the smell of the pond was rank in his nostrils, a pungent sea odor of drowning.

In such fashion Fred MacCann, who was a person and not a thing, capable of independent decision and sensitive to his integrity as a person, made the stations of his Cross.

He moved slowly to the cement rim of the pool and felt its chill against his body.

This is it, he said to himself, slowly. *This is what the booby trap didn't do to me in Sicily. This is that drink of water I wanted. This is it.*

And then with a sharp little cry, he fell over the rim of the pond, into the water. In the shock of its coldness he expelled all the air from his lungs; all of it; then, with a conscious and very specific effort of his will, which was the will of a living and dying *person*, he opened his mouth and inhaled water: for it seemed to him in that moment that he heard running footsteps, footsteps hurrying up the long and rising corridor of his life, and voices calling to him to wait, to consider; telling him that it wasn't as bad as all that, that he hadn't been used at all; that he was a whole person, not a thing; that he had a whole rich life ahead of him, alone in his basket, in his private room, in his fine modern hospital, on the outskirts of Washington, D.C., within easy commuting distance from the Capitol.

Titles in This Series

14 Annette Fiske. *First Fifty Years of the Waltham Training School for Nurses*. New York, 1984. BOUND WITH Alfred Worcester. "The Shortage of Nurses—Reminiscences of Alfred Worcester '83." *Harvard Medical Alumni Bulletin 23*, 1949.

15 Virginia Henderson et al. *Nursing Studies Index, 1900–1959*. Philadelphia, 1963, 1966, 1970, 1972.

16 Darlene Clark Hine, editor. *Black Women in Nursing: An Anthology of Historical Sources*.

17 Ellen N. LaMotte. *The Tuberculosis Nurse*. New York, 1915.

18 Barbara Melosh, editor. *American Nurses in Fiction: An Anthology of Short Stories*.

19 Mary Adelaide Nutting. *A Sound Economic Basis for Schools of Nursing*. New York, 1926.

20 Sara E. Parsons. *Nursing Problems and Obligations*. Boston, 1916.

21 Juanita Redmond. *I Served on Bataan*. Philadelphia, 1943.

22 Susan Reverby, editor. *The East Harlem Health Center Demonstration: An Anthology of Pamphlets*.

23 Isabel Hampton Robb. *Educational Standards for Nurses*. Cleveland, 1907.

24 Sister M. Theophane Shoemaker. *History of Nurse-Midwifery in the United States*. Washington, D.C., 1947.

25 Isabel M. Stewart. *Education of Nurses*. New York, 1943.

26 Virginia S. Thatcher. *History of Anesthesia with Emphasis on the Nurse Specialist*. Philadelphia, 1953.

27 Adah H. Thoms. *Pathfinders—A History of the Progress of Colored Graduate Nurses*. New York, 1929.

28 Clara S. Weeks-Shaw. *A Text-Book of Nursing for the Use of Training Schools, Families, and Private Students*. New York, 1885.

29 Writers Program of the WPA in Kansas, compilers. *Lamps on the Prairie: A History of Nursing in Kansas*. Topeka, 1942.